Marie I

Mieke van Poll

MIEKE VAN POLL

Copyright © 2018 DM van Poll Suykerbuyk
All rights reserved.

ISBN: 9781717990082

MARIE LOUISE

Aan mijn maan

PROLOGUE

The trouble is as follows. People have a set image of the person I am. And that image adds up most of the time, really. But when it doesn't it really does not. For I feel the pressure of living up to what people expect me to be. Letting down the ones I love isn't one of my hobbies as one can imagine. There's a lot at stake. I sometimes feel I am pushed into a life I haven't fully chosen. It fits the picture-perfect life many of us aspire to live. But perfect is never perfect up close. Life isn't a puzzle that magically falls into place. I am sorry to burst that bubble. I truly am. It hurts me more than people think. It's not enjoyable to see those broken faces, those disappointed grins when I tell them what I really want. The only explanation for my actions I can give is a perpetual yearning for change. I am not one to conform to a certain group, a certain path. Do not call me a lost soul, for I know exactly what I want and need but I often try to restrain myself. My body, mind and heart want three different things.

Usually my mind happily takes charge. I feel responsible and happy when that part of me takes over. It's the most desirable way of living, really. I have a reasonable and caring mind. I am smart and practical. I love myself the most when my mind is in charge.

When my heart's in charge I still feel okay. I am a loving person and am perfectly capable of living for others.

The drama sometimes takes over, and that can make me somewhat obnoxious. It annoys me sometimes, and at times like these I long for the simple times when my mind is in charge.
When my body takes the driver's seat the shit will hit the fan. Some people call me a nymphomaniac. I know I am not, for most of the time these other two parts of me control my way of living, but because we can't live in harmony, my body can't be tamed. It's a primitive part of me, a manly part even. And because I am a woman it is explained as nymphomania. My body can take me to great heights, heights higher than the highest buzz anything else can give you.
The trouble is that I can never enjoy the ways of my body with the people I truly love. I need anonymity to fully get into ecstasy. It's when this part of me is in charge that mayhem appears. It's a destructive phase I usually go through. I honestly try to not repress my body's wishes to still keep some control over the brakes, but once every few years the brakes break and that's when I destroy everything I've carefully built. I am a very Catholic girl, and I identify with Eve whenever this happens. I am so fixated on this apple and it really doesn't matter if I do realize that taking the apple can destroy manhood or paradise; that apple must be mine and there's no one who can stop me.

That scares me so much. I truly feel alone during these phases. I know what is coming, I try to hold on to everything I hold dear without any hope of a happy ending. I feel like I am in the dark, and I know exactly where I am heading. I feel the pain of everyone I love on my shoulders, and I try to punish myself. I stop taking care of my body, start drinking, enjoy the hangovers and the pain I feel in my throat of the many cigarettes I am not used to smoking. No one else will ever punish me, even when I come clean before the real mayhem occurs. They just cannot comprehend what I am telling them. That the dusk has fallen, that the lovely girl, woman, mother I am does not know how to turn the tide. 'Choose the right path' is what they keep on repeating. But they obviously do not know what it feels like to have no control over a part of yourself. I usually try to be as honest as words can put it. But I have learned that people will only hear what they want to hear. So here I am, yet again. On the run from my former life. The dusk has gone, the dark has gone, and all there is left is the smoking barrel of the gun that has just gone off. The remains of my former life lie still when I close the door.

Marie Louise, 10-09-1946

CHAPTER ONE

When Marie Louise – or Louise as she would be called later in life – was born, it stormed and thundered in an extremely loud manner. Her mother would forever add that the noise hasn't stopped since. Hardly the truth according to Louise, for she found herself to be a very responsible child. And grown-up, for that matter. Her mother just referred to the tantrums that would occasionally occur. And those outbursts were totally called for. As the oldest daughter of an umbrella factory director in Tilburg, an industrial town in the Catholic south of the Netherlands, Louise did grow up to be a smart and charming girl. But being eldest of three siblings meant having a lot of responsibilities at an early age. And even before Louise was able to read her first word, her parents knew all too well that this strawberry blonde girl was brighter than most of her relatives. She struggled from the start to find anyone who would understand her and what she was saying. And that sometimes tired her, and tiredness made her aggressive. Later on, the aggressiveness slowly grew into something much subtler but also a lot more dangerous: She became a master manipulator.
That came in handy when she was sent off to a Catholic boarding school for girls, a few hours from where her parents lived. And although lots of girls of her age did not want to leave their parents and the life

they knew behind, Louise could not wait to start this new adventure. It did not matter that this adventure meant living at a strict boarding school run by nuns. Louise thought anything new was worth experiencing. The year before she left, she wrote down stories in her journal about how she and other girls would escape through the windows to go about town and get into some trouble. The reality was that Louise was not as mischievous as her stories might have led others to believe. There were times when the butterflies in her stomach made her want to forget about all her manners, and rally up the girls in her dorm to just get up and leave; but then her conscience usually stopped her, for she did not want to hurt the nuns' feelings. As she got older and her hormones started to get the upper hand sometimes, she did get into some trouble. But she had built up enough credits to get away with not making her curfew, or with wearing make-up in class.
Besides being a very charming and caring girl, academically she was like no other girl in school. There were other smart girls in her class, and in some subjects they even got higher grades. But Louise outsmarted them all when it came to exact sciences. Lucky for her for she was not the perfect little scholar. She read books like there was no tomorrow, but as soon as they

were on her obligated reading list, she lost interest. And besides, she did not want to read Dutch books. Because what would perfect Dutch bring her? It was not common for a girl in the 1920's to explore other languages, but Louise had decided a while ago that she would not stay in the Netherlands for the rest of her life. And that's why she read French and English books instead of the obligatory Dutch ones. A solid favourite had to be 'La dame aux Camélias'. She found it hopelessly romantic. Anything that ended in death, longing and despair had Louise at the edge of her seat, she would often tell her fellow classmates. Who in return, would just giggle and tease her with her penchant for drama.

But Louise had a very practical side as well. She aspired to be a doctor. An unthinkable dream for a girl in that era. And although her parents were quite liberal, they did not allow Louise to study medicines. She would be the only girl to attend and besides, who would want to marry her? Their decision on her future devastated her and truly broke her heart, for at least a couple of days. She was never the one to really put up a fight when things got hard. Mainly because she respected and loved her parents, and did not want to hurt their feelings – but maybe more importantly: There were so many other possibilities. So she would not become a doctor. Maybe she would marry one and take off with

him to faraway countries to teach medicine there and help out local communities. She would not need a diploma there, and would attend as a doctor to the patients anyway. Louise was never really fussed when something did not work out the way it should have at first, as that just meant she could think of new and exciting ways to reach her goal: Never be boring.
After boarding school, her parents decided she should help out in her father's factory. Of course she threw a tantrum and swore not to set one foot into the prison that was this factory. But after a couple of weeks Louise managed to happily work her way up to general manager there. She turned out to be an immediate success. Mainly because she found out she liked working. That surprised her parents as much as it surprised her. Given the chance, Louise would rather crawl into her bed or the sofa and hide away with a book for days on end, than to go out for a walk or play any sports. They'd called her Lazy Louise before she started out in the factory. But she discovered that when she had a clear goal, she could stand on her feet for hours on end. She loved doing all sorts of jobs at once. One minute she would attend to a problem in the actual factory, and the next she would crunch the numbers with her uncle. She loved wearing pants and tucking her long hair into a tight bun. All the running around even made her lose some weight, and at the age

of 18, Louise had never looked better.

And she had never felt any better. It was time for her next dream, becoming director of the umbrella factory. As the oldest child of her father, who was first in line to take over the factory, and her younger brother being a terrible choice for a successor, the logical next step would be to leave her in charge. But of course even Louise knew that too would be an unrealistic dream. It would mean that she could not get married, and that was the one thing that never changed in her ever-altering dreams. To be swept away and find the love of her life, to find true passion and romance, to marry and live happily ever after. Louise could not wait. So no matter how much she loved working at the factory, she would never give up true love for anything.

But true love was a tricky thing to find. Louise got distracted from it a couple of times, solely because of the excitement other boys brought with them. She had not been around boys as much as she would have liked. And frankly, the world was a safer place for it. The one time she did encounter a man who was not a relative or friend of her brother's, Louise projected all the moves she had learned from her books she'd read and the plays she had seen with her parents.

She did not know she would have the guts to actually act the way she had done with this man, who happened to be her Latin teacher. She was used to her mind

wandering off to great heights and taking her body with it, but in real life she usually chickened out. Whenever a man or boy came near, she lost interest. But when Mr Gijzen started to teach at her school she was shocked. Shocked, like the rest of her peers and teachers that a school like hers would employ such a young and handsome, male teacher. But also shocked as to what power her body had over her. Ever since he had entered the premises Louise seemed to have one goal. And that was to be alone with him. It spiked up her Latin grades and her interest for anything to do with the Roman Empire. She even tried to read the six volumes of The Decline and Fall of the Roman Empire and although she had put in a solid effort, by the time she came to two thirds of the first part, she had already lost any interest in this young, but rather dull teacher. There was no point in finishing it now, Louise thought bitterly, and exchanged the three thick books for The Undying Fire by H.G. Wells, seeing as though she was a bit fed up with school and teachers at that point.
Before losing interest, Louise did get her way with him. She sneaked out with him on more than one occasion. It never occurred to her to feel guilty or bad about it. Why would she? He was not married and just a few years her senior. But even if there would have been a reason in her mind to feel guilty, there wasn't any time

to think about it. Stunned by what a simple look could do, Louise had just let life wash over her without really thinking about it. It exceeded her expectations, that first encounter with a man. No matter how romantic and dramatic her mind worked, the rational part had prepared her for a long courtship. But instead it seemed that the speed in which the Lord and Ladies wooed each other in her Jane Austen novels was not that fictional after all.

The first time they got together, Louise had subtly eyed him up during one of the school dances. At least that was the way she described their first encounter in her diary. She imagined him being mesmerised by her shy look and strands of her hair coyly falling around her pale face. According to her diary he had immediately understood and taken her into the shed at the back of the garden of the convent. Reading back over these passages as a grown woman, Louise smirked at the interpretation of a young and hormonal girl. In fact she had had to lure him away by telling him that she had spotted a fox in the shed.

She did wonder about his intentions, but the adult Louise understood better than anyone the effect she could have on men. Even at an early age. And besides, Mr Gijzen had been just over 20 years old. He did go on to explain his actions later on to her. He was not the type of man that would take advantage of an innocent

young student. He had explained it a decision his body had made for him; his mind had not had a say in it, for he knew all too well that it was in fact very wrong to take one of his pupils away solely for his pleasure. In fact, at first he had not even dared to kiss her. He had begged her to stop.
"Louise, stop. We should not be doing this. Let us just go back."
"Oh Mr Gijzen, let us just go for it. I am sure God would not have given me this yearning to kiss you just for me to ignore it? Or do you not find me attractive?"
Finally Louise could use the words that her heroines had huskily sighed to their freshly found lovers. This was what it felt like to be alive!
"I do, Louise. Very much so. But I am your teacher. This just feels wrong."
Him denying her at first just made her want him more. Love should never be easy. There should be some sort of fight, some sort of conquest.
"Well, I do not agree. In fact, it feels better than good."
God would never leave her side. This deeply Catholic girl did not make a single decision without consulting her spiritual leader. A surprise to most, for almost anyone would have made other choices with Him in their head. But Louise always had her own views on religion, God and what was right or wrong. He was her companion, her guide through life. And she was very

certain that He wanted her to lead her life using her intuition and sense, and not rules set by men.

"Come Mr Gijzen. Touch me." She giggled.

When he finally grabbed her and leaned in for a kiss her skin felt electric. Every hair in her body had risen and her blood plunged in such a hurry from her head to her legs that for a short while, she was sure she was going to faint. When he kissed her while stroking her strawberry blonde hair, Louise was frantically looking for places to put her hands. She wanted to touch him everywhere at once. His broad shoulders, his chest still safely unexposed, his face, his thick black hair. She was fighting for air and worried again about her health, but was reassured by her shivering body. She enjoyed it so much, this is what being in ecstasy must mean, she thought. When he carried on kissing her neck and collarbone she thrust herself onto his body, and together they crashed onto the floor. She lay on her side to break free from him for just a short moment, and stared him right in the face. That frightened him and he immediately let her go.

"Are you all right, Louise? Why did you stop?"

His face was all pale except for the marks from her pink lipstick she had secretly applied in the dark, when she had followed him to the shed. He panted heavily and started to crawl up when she stopped him.

"I just want to savour the moment," she remembered

saying.

Louise looked into the eyes of the man who had taught her all about Augustus and Brutus, and she felt older already. She realized that when it comes to intimacy a woman is always more powerful. Probably the only time a woman is more powerful than a man. That was the moment she really wanted to savour. She loved the fact that this time she was in charge, and she could decide whether they would or would not go through with it. She smiled and slowly crawled towards him. She made sure not to kiss him on his lips, but proceeded to unbutton his shirt while looking up at him. But not in the way she used to look up at him. This time she was pulling the ropes.

"Are you sure?"

"Sssssh," she replied huskily.

When she was done exposing his chest, she stood up in front of him and took off her dress very slowly. She had borrowed the dress from her friend Gertrude, who was slimmer than she was. Her breasts were therefore pushed up slightly and she was all too aware of that. She saw him looking at her, mesmerised, while she slipped off her dress. The soft chiffon fabric brushed her hips when it fell down, and she was now dressed in nothing but her underwear. But she did not feel naked at all. She had never felt more at ease than at this very moment. Louise stepped out of the little pile of fabric

and draped her body against his chest. She nodded and let him touch her bare skin. When he bent over for a kiss she took off her bra and gently pushed him on his back. She crawled on top of him and started kissing his bare chest. When she reached his trousers she looked up at him once more and smiled. She undid his zipper and slowly removed his pants. She kissed his briefs slowly and crawled up again.
"Now you can have your way with me."
She lay on her back and put her hands behind her head. She smiled when he started kissing her all over, and she kept on smiling until he removed her panties to have his way with her. She closed her eyes for a second and breathed heavily through the initial pain. She lifted up her legs, and after what seemed just a few seconds, she felt him shiver all over. He moaned a few times and fell on top of her. When he looked at her after a while, she felt like she had found out the secret of life.

~

Her first fiancé was a fine man from a city a few kilometres farther down south in the Netherlands. He was a friend of the family and very fond of Louise. They had known each other for ages and Louise trusted him like no other. For some reason she had never really treated him like a boy, or later on, a man. She knew she was not really in love with him, but for some reason she forgot about her oath to fall madly in love. She felt as though she did not have too much time to lose. It had become clear to her that as an unmarried woman she did not have that many options, and at least she trusted Fons to give her the freedom she so yearned for. Her family was happy too. Fons was from a fine family who shared their values and Catholic views. It was a match that seemed to please all involved parties. And Louise liked being in Fons' company. Although she wasn't coy or timid at all, she was impressed by the kind of people Fons introduced her to. He took her to all kinds of gatherings where she would encounter respectable and distinguished people. Definitely not a stranger to merrymakings as her parents loved hosting dinner parties like no other family in Tilburg. But their guests usually were other factory owners, and once every blue moon the mayor came by for a cup of tea. The people Fons introduced her to were almost royalty, or at least they came across that way. Louise felt right at home. Not because she was into appearances – she was not at all really – but because these people usually had seen so much more than she had. These were the Roaring Twenties, and there was no limit as to what was possible. Aeroplanes were not used solely for fighting anymore. Charles Lindbergh had crossed the Atlantic Ocean just two years prior, and many more adventurous pilots followed afterwards. Passenger flights were no longer a Utopia. Holidays to America and cruises to Australia became the fashion. And Louise was intrigued. She wanted to experience everything everywhere. So far she had only seen France, Germany and Belgium – which was not a too bad travelling experience for a girl her age in that time. Her parents loved going on holidays. It meant that they could take their Leica with them. Making photos was an expensive hobby but Louise and her parents were well-off, so they could afford to capture their adventures abroad. Louise's visits to France and Germany had left her wanting more. She dreamed of exotic places and handsome men who would show her the way.

Men to Louise were more than objects of lust, they were her gateway to a better life. That trait alone did not make her stand out in a crowd. Many girls knew that their chances in life were heavily linked to the man they were to marry. The fact that Louise could not imagine just picking out one to spend the rest of her life with was what made her a bit odd from time to time. She was completely frank about it, which made anyone around her kind of uncomfortable. Her parents were convinced it was just her age. Other, less liberal souls blamed the literature Louise had been reading from an early age. A lot of the novels had not been translated into Dutch, so no one exactly knew what she was reading.

Unfazed by any of the snide comments Louise received when rolling out her plans, she carried on her new role as worldly fiancée soon to be wife of Fons. He had already been helping her to expand her horizons. In the few months she had spent as his fiancée, she had seen and heard more about life than she had in the 19 years before being his. And what she had not expected beforehand: She enjoyed being someone's girl in every possible way. Of course she enjoyed the physical aspect of being in a steady relationship, even though she did wonder if she had not interpreted God's path for her too freely by consummating a relationship before she was legally married, but she shushed her conscience by telling it she was sure God would not have given her this urge to be led on by her bodily wishes.

But more importantly, she discovered a lot about herself by simply being someone's girlfriend. There was this other urge that grew stronger as their relationship progressed. She found out that she loved to take care of Fons. All of a sudden her mother forcing cooking lessons onto her did not cause as much mayhem as before. She even began to look for foreign recipe books during her monthly visits to several flea markets, looking for foreign books. She even picked up a British book for housewives, the articles describing how to find your own home decoration style. It would always come in handy, Louise thought. She had never expected this side of her to appear. Of course, as an older sister she had always felt responsible, and maybe even tempted to take care of her younger siblings from time to time, but her lazy nature stopped her from really following through her aspirations to be a true surrogate mother. To be honest, these urges only appeared after reading about strong, independent women with a child, which made their heroism even more admirable. Not a stranger to making fun of herself and the countless plans she had made for herself, it was incredibly funny that this softer side appeared without no actual motive. And like always, whenever Louise saw the purpose of perfecting certain skills, she would do anything in her power to do so.

And boy was there a purpose. It surprised her, the simplicity of men. These creatures who had conquered multiple worlds, invented machines with unlimited possibilities, and had written the most incredible stories that had lasted more than one lifetime, how could they be so incredibly simple? It was like opening a steel fort with numerous safeguards and extra locks by just saying: I want to come in. No matter how intelligent, strong or creative, as long as one was able to feed them and give them some physical attention, every man's shell would crack open like an egg tapped with a butter knife. That knowledge dazzled and disappointed her at the same time. She had expected more. After all it was men that had introduced her to the most magical secrets in the world. How was it possible that they were so easily manipulated?

Shakespeare had taught her about the complexity of relationships, Pythagoras had shown her how to do wonderful things with numbers, and she had a special interest in anything Descartes had to teach her about the power of the mind over the body. A theory that frankly made her insecure. Because somehow she was never really strong enough to ignore the weaknesses of the body, and rely solely on the infinite power of her mind. 'Cogito, ergo sum' on good days, she sometimes sighed and started to wonder if Descartes himself had ever been served the way Fons had by Louise. Maybe his mind would not be as powerful anymore, Louise thought bitterly to soothe her own shortcomings.

Yet ever since she had been with Fons, she'd had less trouble overpowering her body, and that soothed her and affirmed her decision to marry Fons, although not in love. It was the sensible thing to do.

CHAPTER TWO

Louise met August on a Saturday evening during a big event in Roosendaal, the village August was born and raised in. He was a friend of her fiancé Fons, and seemed thrilled to finally meet this girl his friend would not stop talking about. Immediately he stirred something in Louise's posture. Instead of greeting him in her usual charming way, her ankles gave in and she stumbled in his direction, pointing her hand at his stomach instead of his hand to shake it. It had not been his overall handsome looks that affected Louise's behaviour. His thick black glasses and his thin frame made him look somewhat like a scatterbrain. But his eyes could easily make you forget your troubles. He had an incredibly kind face, and when he smiled Louise could not find a hint of bitterness in his ever so blue eyes. In fact August had little to be bitter about. Louise later on added to her memory. Growing up in the warm family he had been blessed with, gave him an extremely bright view on life, and all that was on offer. His father Charles, a charming and welcoming man Louise thought, had raised his son to be a successor of the printing business he had inherited from his own father. He had done so in a kind and loving manner and ensured August to be kind and generous to his staff. Charles was known for his excellent people skills. His son lacked some of his natural charm, much to her delight. Instead of relying on what God had given him, like his father, August had to work hard to gain the respect of his staff, clients and of course Louise. But not without any success. August too was a hard worker and turned out to be even better for his staff and business than his father was.

August was practically raised by his father as his mother had been ill for a long time, and died when August was still in his teens. Louise thought it to be a remarkable relationship, the one Charles and August shared. She had never seen a father so doting. Especially not when it concerned a son. Later on, she turned out to be eternally grateful for this great example Charles had set. August was perfectly equipped for the job she would unwillingly force upon him, much later on.

There was just one stain on the father-son bond, and that stain was called Ilda. After August's mother died, Charles wanted to find him a suitable mother soon, but instead married a German woman no one tended to like. Although Ilda was not as forthcoming as August had hoped for, he still gave her a chance like he would give everyone a chance.

When August met Louise that night he had already taken over a part of his father's printing business. At the same time he just had been appointed president of the local theatre where the party was held. A logical position, for August was very much interested in anything cultural. Being the president of the local theatre meant he would be able to bring the cultural standard in Roosendaal to a higher level. Something he desperately longed for. He had his life all worked out at the age of 24. And was even about to get married to his long-time girlfriend, Anna. Until he met Louise.

She remembered how he visibly struggled internally. Should he talk to her or should he stay far away from her, just to be safe? Descartes lost this time, she chuckled to herself when August turned to her and stuttered:

"What do you think of the party? Anything like the ones you are used to?"

Louise turned to August and gazed sweetly into his eyes.

"Well sir. Or shall I call you August? I think this is one of the most exquisite parties Fons has ever taken me to."

She played coy. Very well aware of that being the right tactic to woo this man. Not sure as to why she needed to impress this man.

He had seemed to find his posture again and bellowed:

"Please Louise, call me August! And let me tell you, I for one am thrilled to have you both here."

He grabbed onto Fons as if he were looking for a strong shoulder to hang on to, and excused himself to get some drinks for the three of them. A tad disappointed, Louise turned to Fons and tried to start a conversation when August returned with a tray clattering with drinks. His nervousness strengthened her suspicions and she decided to resume her pursuit of August. But the mere thrill of shooting the deer turned out to be far less interesting than the actual deer. Louise was truly excited about this man.

She asked him all about his new position and hung on to his every word when he told her about his business. It was so exciting to meet a man of her age and her class to have a goal of his own. Most of the men in her circle were born wealthy and were less ambitious. August was quite the opposite. He told her all about the plans he had for expanding the printing business. He wanted more than to just print papers, he wanted to create them as well. Louise imagined supporting his ambitions. She knew she had the skills to make his dreams come true. She snapped back to reality when he asked her a question.

"Louise, I have to ask you. What kind of music do you like?"

Clever as ever, Louise knew that this was not a random question to keep their conversation going. They had been talking without any difficulties or awkward pauses. She knew this must be another passion of his. So she decided to impress him with her knowledge of a very new sort of music: Jazz.

"Mainly contemporary music I suppose. I am really liking Jazz at the moment. The music blacks in New Orleans and Chicago make?"

Later on, Louise of course found out August had a great love for opera. Unfortunately for his loved ones he was especially fond of the heavyweight composer Richard Wagner, and found all lighter operas and operettas trivial. Her so-called love for Jazz gave him fuming headaches, even more so when he discovered his eldest and highly musically talented son had a deep passion for this improv music. A passion so deep he would give up everything to become a successful Jazz-pianist.

But at that moment all that August heard was the wisdom of the young Louise. There were several years between them but she knew so much already. She seemed to be interested far beyond the normalities of life. And there was no doubt about it, Louise knew he found her to be an attractive girl. This evening she had put up her curly strawberry blonde hair in a loose bun with little strays to frame her round face. She had kept her make-up from hiding her freckles, because she knew they made her look carefree and young, a much-needed look, for people always thought she was much older than she actually was. Looking back, Louise gathered she must have had an unusual elegance about

her, especially considering how old she then was. All this helped August to fall in love with her. With the added flattery of her hanging onto his every word, the deal was basically sealed. Without an agenda this time she encouraged him to tell her everything about operas, plays, books and even where he had gone on holidays.
"So your car was lifted upon an actual ferry?" she had asked him in awe when he had told her about his holiday to North Cornwall.
"Well yes, they have converted some of the older ships into car ferries now. Father was thrilled to drive his own car to England. He hates driving in strange cars."
He had gone to England with his father, his father's new wife and his little sister, he went on telling her. Then the party of four had proceeded to drive cross country and after three days they had finally arrived in Bude, North Cornwall. He said he had never seen such beauty in all his life.
"Until you met me," was her cheeky reply.
From then on something changed in the way they spoke to one another, Louise noticed. He went on telling her about the green hills, the sheep with black heads and how much he had recognised from the novels he had read, but he could not concentrate well on the stories he was telling her. He kept on losing his train of thought and repeating sentences, which she found extremely adorable. It made her shy and girly in

front of him, causing her to curl her hair around her finger and softly swing her hips from side to side. She noticed him staring at her red dress and her subtle cleavage. She decided against making an obvious move towards him, but instead let her body speak. Louise had looked down slightly so that she had to look at him from under her eyelashes. She knew she was getting to him, as every time she would bite her lip he would shiver slightly and stumble on his words.

"I am sorry. Have I made you nervous?" she asked earnestly.

"To be quite honest, yes madam you have."

Louise had learned a lot since the first time she had seduced her Latin teacher. However, Fons did not need a lot of persuasion – for he was very much enamoured with her already – Louise had worked her magic on him on more than one occasion. It had become a sport of some sorts. A sport she was good at for once. And she was moving on to the next league right now. Not only because August was a respectable man with an even more respectable future, but because he was an interesting man. A bright and promising man, yet with no excessive pride or arrogance. She immediately fell for August in a way she had not fallen for anyone before. This is what it felt like, she instantly sighed, to be in love.

Although Louise had come with Fons and August was

about to marry his long-time girl Anna, without saying it out loud, both August and Louise decided then and there that they would leave the party as a couple. August would afterwards describe their encounter as a life-altering one, and to him it certainly was. He would never love a woman as much as he loved her, and he proved so immediately by ending his engagement to Anna. For August, although he was a self-proclaimed romantic, this meant an out-of-character move. He was never the person to break his promises. Though it would not be the last time that he would break his vows, it would be the last time he would break them voluntarily.

~

For Louise, breaking up with Fons wasn't much of a challenge. He had already seen the look upon her face when she first met August, and had already secretly decided beforehand that she could never be the girl he would marry. They were after all more friends than lovers, and from a very early stage in their relationship he had realised he would not be able to make her happy in the long run. At least that is what he told her when she broke the news to him. Louise was quite relieved to have split from Fons amicably, and very pleased to hear from him that he too had met a girl he was much more in love with. Later on, the pair of them would tell people that staying friends after their broken engagement was the best thing they had ever decided upon, although their two-year engagement had brought them both lots of joy.

Fons told her he admired August just as much as she did, and he thought them to be a good match; he also told this to her somewhat confused parents. They were not as pleased as the former couple, for a broken engagement was an enormous scandal at that time. Especially a public one like theirs. But they handled this fact graciously and like proper adults, and that seemed to limit the reputational damage.

August was less thrilled about his broken engagement, Louise knew. Although he had been unable to wipe the smile from his face, he explained, the harsh reality of having to hurt someone he cared for very much made him come off his cloud nine for a short while. He did not like the man he was looking at in the mirror in the mornings, although he could not help but smile when thinking that soon this man would be Louise's. She had put a lot of weight onto this sentence, for it was practically a proposal. He told his future wife that he counted his blessings every day, all the while equally praying for forgiveness. August was a very Catholic man like Louise, but unlike her he was determined to obey the rules the Catholic Church had set for him. He did not think God would forgive his sins when they were an immediate outcome of his nature. He sometimes pondered for days on end about what God's intentions were, and in what way he should be living his life in order to be a good Catholic. He did not ponder long about this matter though, for he was sure that God most definitely thought breaking off an engagement to be a sin. Whenever he spoke to Louise about the matter she laughed, stroked his hair and told him God had intended for them to be together; and that it showed character that he had done something very difficult in order to get what was obviously in the stars. She made it sound like there was no other explanation.

~

Her insatiable thirst for all the secrets the world had to offer mesmerised August, and Louise was flattered that a man with his knowledge thought she was intelligent and worldly. He often told her that no other woman he knew, or man for that matter, knew this much trivia, literature, science and gossip all at once. August did not know where she had gotten all that knowledge, for he was sure that the nuns at the boarding school she had attended had never heard of most things she told him. Whenever he asked her about where she had gotten all those stories and facts, she would smile coyly and say that she just liked to listen. Which was true. Anyone who had anything to add got the time of day from Louise. She did not care for ranks, age or education, as long as someone was an enticing storyteller. And with August she had found a true match. On the surface August was the silent, obedient one in the relationship, whereas Louise would have been described as a woman one could not ignore, and therefore rarely known for her great listening skills. But in fact she was a great listener, and that trait made her very loved by anyone August introduced her to.

His father first and foremost could not get over the fact that his son had found such a beautiful and lovely wife. He had liked Anna, he had confessed to her once, but he found Louise to be somewhat of a rarer breed. He always joked that his daughter-in-law was the centre of attention. In a good way. She guessed her excitement and wit and ability to turn every dinner into a memorable evening was the main reason for this praise. Throwing a good dinner party was very much appreciated in the printer's household, for entertaining was one the family's favourite pastimes. And not only did Louise know how to enchant a room full of people by just being herself, but her relationship with Fons had turned her into a perfect cook. Being fluent in French gave her the option of cooking from modern French cookbooks, which she had found browsing for one of her foreign novels at the flea markets. She had even bought one in Provence when she vacationed with her parents a year before. Her dishes were full of exotic herb mixes and of course she would top off her dinners with her specialty: desserts. Puddings, custards, meringues, she made it all from scratch. Needless to say, both men very much enjoyed these skills. She loved spoiling August and his father just as well, and loved the prospect of throwing dinner parties as a family. Especially when she thought of the beautiful townhouse she was about to live in with August.

Roosendaal had a small town centre but the houses that circled the town square were spacious and well kept. Louise's future home had an enormous entrance which led to an ancient staircase. At the back of the property

there was a decent-sized garden with a separate home for the servants. Apart from the huge kitchen, the first floor had a spacious study filled with August's books and paintings, and a reception room that was welcoming and white. Upstairs there were two bathrooms and four bedrooms. She could not wait to put her mark on the house. August had told her she had carte blanche to change any furniture in the rooms. Although she'd grown up in a wealthy family and would soon marry into an even wealthier one, she had never had many material wishes. Sure, she dressed in the latest fashion and had more shoes than any other woman in Roosendaal, but she never asked for a thing. She was an excellent seamstress and could easily make her own clothing. So she was not planning on changing the entire house just for the sake of it. However, she could not wait to modernize the kitchen. So one day, when she was visiting August for the last time before their wedding, she did ask her husband for a grand investment.
"August darling. I have a great big favour to ask you, I am afraid."
August looked up from his book, a Russian author no doubt as he was really into them around that time, and looked directly at her. He still did that at the beginning of their courtship. After a while he was less prone to drop everything at the drop of a hat to listen to his

wife. It wasn't a lack of interest but more of natural decay of a relationship between two people, Louise thought. He would until the very end find everything she said important. Maybe he looked at her still because of her longer strawberry blonde hair. She was growing out her shorter locks for the wedding. Back in the day she had really put an effort into her looks whenever she would meet him. Her dress that day was unlike any other ever seen on the streets of Roosendaal. She had sown shoulder pads into her dresses to make her waists look smaller. Most of her dresses were floral back then. At that time Louise claimed it to be all the rage in France and America, not caring at all that no one else in Roosendaal wore similar clothing.

"Do tell me, my dear. What is the matter? Everything all right?"

She replied quickly, feeling some impatience bubbling up. She could not quite figure out why, but sometimes his forever-calm manner irritated her already.

"Certainly, darling. I was just wondering. With us getting married and living together and all, we will probably entertain a lot of guests, right?"

August nodded with a smile.

"And when we do entertain guests, I will do most of the cooking, isn't that so?"

She adjusted her tone, for she was about to ask him for quite an investment and did not want to come across spoiled or ungrateful.

"That sounds like a wonderful future, my dear."

She lost her calm tone again and sighed:

"Well yes, darling, I agree. But the stove you have in the kitchen at the moment... It isn't really up to modern standards."

He did not seem to notice or mind her impatience, and he replied gently.

"O but that just will not do. Let's fix that for you, shall we? What kind of stove would you like, my dearest?"

Don't think, just say it, she muttered to herself before hastily blurting out:

"An AGA stove, dear. I would love an AGA stove."

August was quite taken aback with that answer, she immediately noticed, for it was a very expensive stove indeed. Even for August, who did not have to worry about money ever. The reason for its high price was not only the fact that it was an exclusive appliance, but also that the stove was solely made in Britain. So if he would decide to purchase one, he had to order one from England, which made things even more costly.

"Let me think about it, Louise." His face crinkled up like it often did when he was uncomfortable with a situation.

"You will get a new stove, I promise. But I can't promise you an AGA yet."

Louise was slightly embarrassed. She did not mean to

ask for something so expensive. She had read about the stove in a magazine and thought it would fit perfectly in their home. She had never really asked for anything from anyone. Being dependent on anyone was something she wanted to avoid at all costs. But she felt at ease with August and more importantly, she felt she was his equal.

"Of course, my love, look into the prices first. I totally understand."

His response had thrown her off a bit, and she retreated to the reception room, where she would wait for her parents to pick her up for her last week at home.

Much to her delight, her father-in-law, who was sitting in the reception room to accompany his son to the factory as soon as Louise left, had overheard their conversation and was shaking his head in dismay.

"August, would you mind coming in here?"

Charles explained to the stunned young August that he had decided to order an AGA then and there – with his son's money.

"Have you noticed that your future wife is totally out of sorts after your little conversation back there? And for what? You don't need to worry about money at all!"

He continued barking at his son:

"When a girl that wonderful and who can cook that perfectly, asks you for an AGA stove, you will give her an AGA stove," was all he said after August asked his father for an explanation.

When Louise came back after her honeymoon, the AGA was set up and ready in the kitchen she could now call her own.

And from then on August had never refused Louise anything in her life.

CHAPTER THREE

So this is the day every girl dreams of. The best day of one's life, many say. It feels like a lot of pressure put on one single day. But still, it seems to be a true cliché, Louise felt. She stood in her dress and felt all her former doubts wash away. She traced the lace with her hands and looked closely at the embroidered details on her veil. Her strawberry blonde hair she had tucked back into a low bun with some stray hairs in curly strings around her face. She looked radiant. She did not feel as nervous as she had expected to be, but became more impatient every minute. She worried that she would break out in a sweat and ruin the tight sleeves. Although she was born midsummer, her body seemed ill-equipped against the warmth that filled the hall of the normally cool church. She had waited until the very last minute to put on her dress. She was known to spill on anything she just put on, and on a nervous day like this the likeliness of spilling increased.

But as she stood there waiting for the first notes of Wagner's bridal chorus to fill the room, she wondered if it would have been inappropriate to wait even longer, and to just put on her dress right here in this hall. Louise chuckled. She often wondered if others laughed at their own jokes as often as she secretly did. Whenever she was nervous or bored she tried to have fun with her own mind, and usually succeeded. She would never tell anyone of course; she already had a lot of explaining to do about her character without confessing that she found herself better company than she found anyone else.

She shook her head at her own thoughts and started pacing around the room. She could never stand up quite so long. Not the best trade for a Catholic girl, since it was the custom to stand throughout long parts of the Mass, including during the Gospel. Pacing through a tiny little hall with an enormous train proved to be a challenge, and when she tripped over her own feet for the third time in half a minute she decided to stop. She was starting to perspire anyway. When finally the heavy tones of the organ resounded through the enormous space, the doors of the church opened and there stood August. She had never seen him look so handsome. He looked downright dashing in his morning jacket and neatly combed hair. She nervously got a hold on his hand and supported herself on him a little as they strode towards the altar. Although Louise was seen as a lady of class she was also a little clumsy and would fall down easily. "Weak ankles," her mother used to sigh when Louise came home with holes in her dresses again. She wasn't a tomboy at all, but simply had trouble walking on uneven roads. And in Tilburg in the 1920's an even road was a rarity. It did not prevent her from wearing heels though. And even now, well into her twenties, she seldom survived a week without tripping and falling down in the street. She was not planning on tripping on her wedding day, though, and had decided to go for flat shoes after all. Her dress basically had a train the size of the aisle of the church, so her shoes would only show when they peeked out from the front. A flat shoe would not be the end of the world, she sternly had told herself many times. She was glad she had been so persuasive. Even in flat shoes she needed the support from her soon-to-be husband. Her ankles felt like rubber in the massive dress. The weight of the fabric, the warmth of the sun coming through the church windows, it all seemed to have an effect on her walking. It was as though a filter for all impulses had been taken away. She heard every squeak of every bench that moved, every mumble, every sneeze ten times as loud as usual. When she looked at August she noticed he was clenching his teeth, for his jawline for once was very visible. Usually he had a soft, round face but right now his features were stern. He turned his head towards Louise and mouthed: "Are you all right?" She charmingly nodded and stroked his elbow. When they reached the aisle Louise was pleased to see the bishop pointing towards the bench in the middle of the church. She had not been to a lot of weddings in the past few years, and did not remember whether the bride and groom were allowed to sit during the ceremony. Fortunately, they were; she did not know that she would have been able to stand for another hour without collapsing to the floor.

And then she was married. Just like that. It seemed odd that a life-altering event could happen in just a few seconds. She had half expected the world to shift for a minute, but it did not. She did not even feel her heart jump or her spine shiver. They said I do and that was it. Of course she knew this beforehand, but the romantic in her had braced Louise for tears, goose bumps or something of that sort. To say she was disappointed would be too strong a statement, but she had expected more. The rest of the day went by in a flash. That night she stayed at her husband's, she was not used to saying 'husband' yet, home in Roosendaal. As he carried her up the stairs she looked him in the eye. The friendliest blue eyes a girl could ever come across. She laughed so hard when he hit her head on the banister that she hit her head again, but now her own doing. She had never felt so comfortable with someone as with August, and their wedding night did not alter this feeling. Better yet, as his wife she felt even more loved and safe. O how proud August was of his new wife and her beautiful dress. He had not let her out of sight for one minute. Louise, always happy to be the centre of attention, enjoyed every second of her wedding and found it hard to accept when August told her the night was really over. She had stubbornly asked him for another hour, but he had simply shaken his head. Home would be the next stop. Her new home to be exact.

When they had finally gotten up the stairs without any more injuries or salvos of laughter, it was time to really start their lives together. And although Louise was no stranger when it came to the physical traits of a man, when it came to the way August's body worked she was completely in the dark. She had tried to seduce him before their wedding night, but although August seemed a soft and sometimes even spineless man, Louise had come to know him as everything but spineless. Gentle and soft, most certainly. Spineless and a pushover, never. August knew far too well what he wanted in life, and was self-assured enough to love a woman who craved freedom in speech, mind and decision-making. But that did not mean that she was inclined to make any kind of decisions for him. And having intercourse before marriage was just something August would never do. Like Louise, he was a true Catholic but in contrary to her approach, he was very strict in the customs and the rules of the Church. No matter how hard she had tried to seduce him, August would not cave in. It had made her feel insecure many times. How could he be able to resist her and refuse to love her fully before they got married? Did he not find her attractive? Was there no desire on his part? Because she for one could not wait to get her hands on him. She did not doubt him as a good lover. He was so concerned with her wellbeing and wanted her to be comfortable all times, she was positive this would translate well in their marital bed. She had often imagined how he would have his way with her. How he would gently lift her up and softly put her on the bed. How he would then stroke her hair and trace his hands along her chin, neck, the side of her chest, barely touching her nipple through the fabric of her bra, farther down towards her stomach. She would shiver just thinking of how he would cherish and hold her all through that first night. Never did it come to mind that it was his first time ever to have sexual intercourse, and that it would really come down to nothing more than consummating their marriage.

"Darling, don't you think it would be easier for me to take off my dress first?"

They had been kissing each other frantically for hours, or so it felt to Louise. And still nothing of meaning had really happened. Louise's chin felt red from the tiny stubble that had already grown back a little since this morning's shave on August's face. As soon as they had entered the bedroom, August had grabbed his wife and started kissing her like a maniac. At first she thought it to be passionate and exciting, but after ten minutes Louise was exhausted. It felt as though he did not know what to do next. They were still standing next to their bed. Her dress was far too big to lie in and August did seem to realise that taking the dress off was an option. When Louise really had no patience left at all, she suggested she take the damn thing off. August stopped abruptly as if to say: well, why didn't you think of that sooner? And he uncomfortably watched her get undressed. She struggled with the enormous heap of fabric, but August did not lend a hand. She was too stubborn to ask for his help and spent ages on opening the endless row of buttons and zippers. When she finally was freed from the gorgeous tent that was her wedding dress, she immediately started on her corset. She was not about to repeat this whole scene again, and decided to get rid of anything that would get in the way of August and her body. August fiddled with his hands while he watched her undress completely. He seemed to be at an extreme loss. His eyes were wide open and displayed an amount of panic that Louise had never seen before in a man. At last he managed to get himself together and started to undress himself too. Louise bitterly noted that he could have easily won the Olympics that night for fastest undresser in the entire universe. He jumped into bed with his underpants still on and shivered before he pulled back the blanket, and patted the mattress as an invitation to his wife. Louise's feet seemed to be glued to the floor she had been standing on for the last 15 minutes, and she did not fully realise she was stark naked. Not until she saw that August's eyes were forcefully staring at the mattress he was lying on. She laughed at the ridiculous sight, which thankfully lifted both their spirits. As a result she climbed into bed next to August. Until then she had always expected him to take the lead in the bedroom. But here and now she realised she was the more experienced one, and she needed to guide him. She threw him an all-knowing smile and slowly crawled towards her husband. She stared deep into his eyes and stroked his nose with her index finger. She pushed her lower body against his and she saw him relax. He even moaned a little. Gently she put her lips against his and used her tongue to tickle his lips. She then let her hands run freely over his chest and finally grabbed his hand. She guided his hand to her neck and pushed it farther onto her chest. Next she laid his hand on her bosom and looked at him without blinking. His pupils widened again and his breathing turned into shallow panting within seconds. She gently pushed him onto his back with that same hand, his hand still lying on her chest. Then she threw her legs around his waist, swiftly removed his underpants and slowly moved her hips back and forth. When she bent over to kiss him with her eyes closed, she suddenly felt him shaking all over. She quickly opened her eyes and saw that his were once again wide open, he apologised…and before she knew it she felt a warm stream of fluid against the inside of her thigh. In a first reaction she let her body fall on his and put her head next to his. "It's all right," she whispered. After a while she rolled back to her side of the bed, got out and walked to the bathroom, still naked. She cleaned her thigh with some toilet paper and sighed. A tiny tear formed in the corner of her eye. She shook her head and headed back to the bedroom. August seemed fast asleep. His heavy breathing soon developed into a loud snore. She crawled in clumsily and turned her back to him. "So this is what it's like to be married," she whispered, and fell into a restless dream.

~

At first, life was good for both of the young lovers. Their marriage seemed to become a happy one. But there was something that was eating Louise. Something Louise regretted deeply, for August was a fine man and she was a happier person with him. But after their honeymoon it had become painfully clear that August could not please her in every way possible.

When they had first started to see each other, he seemed to want nothing more than to kiss and touch her. He refused to do the latter before they were married and although Louise herself was not inexperienced in that department, she decided not to defy his wish to wait until they were legally married. She was fairly sure he would know how to love her properly based on the way he kissed her. He kissed with a great passion and often left her longing for more. So when he could not consummate their marriage on their wedding night, Louise was not worried yet. It had been an exhausting day and he had been waiting for such a long time, the pressure must have worked against him. But it wasn't the pressure that kept him from performing. August knew that all too well. Much later on he had confessed this to Louise. He had never been a very physical person. He preferred intellectual satisfactions over physical ones. Besides that he had always found it difficult to look at women he admired as sexual human beings. To him, Louise was every bit a saint, and when she took off her clothes ready to turn into a sexual human being, frankly, it turned him off. He did not want to look at her in that way. He wanted to keep the angelic image he had of her and found it increasingly difficult to touch her wanting body. They worried him, these thoughts that kept him from consummating his marriage. For he was no fool and knew all too well that Louise was a very physical and sexual woman. He told her that he was touched by the way she had handled the situation on their wedding night – by immediately setting his mind at ease by blaming the busy and tiring day. He was not all too sure she believed her own explanation, but he prayed she did.

The following day at the start of their honeymoon he had been determined to show her he could satisfy her in the bedroom too. He'd grabbed her as soon as they were alone in their hotel room. He had kissed her like he had not seen her in ages, and frantically closed his eyes to fight off the image of her perfect soft body in red defiant lingerie. He tried to let go of all his thoughts and doubts and let his body do all the work. But it was hard to overcome the pressure of pleasing her. She was an adventurous type, and by the way she was kissing and touching him back he felt she was no stranger to this game, and he most certainly was.

Another wave of doubt came over him and he nearly lost the fight with his own body. But eventually she knew how to mute the noise in his head by doing exactly what his body needed.
She felt him relax as soon as she laid him down on the bed and stroked his back soothingly.
"Don't you worry, my love. We are married now. There's no need to be in any hurry. Just enjoy my company like I enjoy yours. I am all yours now and you can have me any way you like."
"Oh, Louise. Do not ever think that I consider you as mine. You cannot belong to anyone but yourself. You are an exquisite woman and I do not want to abase you to merely a body just because you are mine by law."
Louise looked at him admiringly. At last she had found someone who appreciated her for her what she was worth. Not because she was a woman, not because she was born into a wealthy family or for any other factors she did not have an influence on. He loved her for the person she was. But this speech had also made it perfectly clear to her that during sex he had difficulties with letting go of the perfect image he had of her. She had recently read about this psychological complex and was intrigued. She was easily intrigued when it came to matters of such sorts, but whatever Freud wrote immediately got her attention for some reason.
"August darling. Shall we turn off the lights and let our

senses do the job?"

She turned off the lights and slowly rolled his warm body towards her, and looked him in the eyes. She smiled and when she squinted her eyes she could still see the relief fill his blue eyes. He kissed her once more, much more softly this time and slowly began to undress her. When he was totally at ease she crawled on top of him and thus, with a few short breaths they consummated their marriage.

August was now relaxed, Louise felt, probably as he had fulfilled his duty as a husband. He had seemed happy, almost arrogantly so, thinking that now she had nothing to worry about. Little did he know that he had just made things worse. Louise was not assured one little bit. She felt all too well that August had worked very hard to please her, but he was not answering his own desires. She thought about the theory she had read once more, and tried to remember if the condition was a permanent one or if most patients would heal after being married a few weeks. She needed it to be the latter. A sexless marriage would be her version of hell. She had found that out in the months before her wedding. It had cost her a great effort to withhold sex for so long. More of an effort than she had imagined beforehand. She did manage to get by because she was longing for his touch, and she convinced herself that she would get a greater gratification by postponing sexual intercourse. She could not have been more off from the truth. Her first sexual experience with her husband was far from satisfactory.

~

Her wedding band had already formed a mark on her ring finger. Even just after a few weeks, the marks of her marriage seemed to have left a definite imprint on her skin. She had read about the first period after a wedding, in novels often described as the most intense and wonderful time of one's life. Louise wondered if she was an exception to the rule. She rubbed her skin in the hope for the deep form of the band to slowly disappear, and decided to take off her ring for the night. Just to see if her finger would return to normal, to the way it was when she was truly and utterly happy with the man she had vowed to stay with forever. She had thought long and hard about why everything had changed the minute they had promised each other eternity. Had it been his confidence about their bond? He seemed so much more at ease after the wedding. As if he had let himself believe she was now finally truly his. He had always been afraid of her leaving him, but now that they were legally man and wife, no one could take her away from him. He seemed calm and happy. And the happier he seemed, the more miserable Louise felt. Why could she not share his happiness? Nothing much had changed. Not in the way they interacted. Even their lives hadn't changed that much. But his puppy-like eagerness irritated her. And his dependence on her pressed heavily on her shoulders. She had involuntary become responsible for the way he felt. It seemed logical, but she knew she didn't need him to feel happy or whole. She loved him for who he was, not for how he made her feel. She would never put such a burden on someone. And although she did not blame him for needing her, she felt trapped most of the time. She was now part of a duo, a synergetic, cooperating organism, never to function separately. She had never realised this beforehand. In her mind marriage was a next stop, not a final destination. August seemed to have found his safe haven and felt certain there was no need for striving for anything beyond this. He and Louise would face life together for as long as they both would live. Forever seemed an awfully long period of time all of a sudden. It had sounded romantic and passionate beforehand, not at all suffocating or daunting. But the everyday reality made her fear the future. Surely all her days would not be like these? They weren't bad, they were good even. But the harsh realisation of the repetitious future seemed tedious at best. Louise had never cared for steadiness. She needed adventures, unexpected endeavours, and crazy passion. And something told her marriage was not going to provide her any of those key elements of living. But she couldn't quite figure out what she was missing. She had hit the jackpot with August. He was one of the few men who weren't afraid to let her live her life the way she liked. He encouraged her to explore her talents, wasn't suspicious when she would meet up with male friends, he could not care less when people would gossip about her. Next to that he was a kind and very wise man. But he did not seem to entice her the way he used to. When they'd first started seeing each other, she had been in awe of all his experience and knowledge. There seemed to be no subject he had not read about. His knowledge had no limits, she used to think. But now she felt she had already come to the Y in the encyclopaedia. He had shared the biggest portion of his wisdom already, and he wasn't interested in expanding his library of facts and stories. He was a content man. He hadn't gathered all that information just to impress her or anyone else. He had truly been interested. But now he seemed to have reached his goal, and unlike her he had no need for setting a new one. She knew she could never live like that. Reaching a goal had proven to be problematic before. She just did not function without having something to strive for. Her everlasting hunger for more would not be stilled soon. In fact, she felt she would never feel truly satisfied. This did not mean in any way she was not happy with her current life, but the voice in her head, warning her of impending agitation along the road, would not quiet down. She despised the little devil talking in her head. How dare he sabotage her newlywed life? How dare he take away the happiness she should have felt during her honeymoon? He did not only affect her and her marriage, but August's life too, although August did not seem to notice the shift in her mood. She was still the caring and loving woman he had met. She had always been mistaken for a sweet and caring kind of person. Louise had never understood this seemingly widely acknowledged perception of her character. She did not find herself a sweet person at all. She wished she was, honestly. But her destructive and aggressive ways sometimes erased every kind gesture she had ever made. She was afraid this time was no exception and that scared her. Even more so than before. For she knew she would not only cause pain and trouble when her destructive self would rear its ugly head. No, this time she would truly damage someone for the rest of his life. That thought was too intense for it to truly sink in. She therefore decided to hold that thought a little longer, and returned to the cupboard where she had put her wedding band, and she shoved it back onto her finger. She turned the small gold ring and polished it with her nightgown. It had already become greasy and matte. After she had rubbed it with the delicate fabric of her nightgown, a faint shine returned. She sighed and retired to the bedroom, where August was already asleep. She hovered above his face and softly stroked his hair. Quietly she turned down the sheets on her side of the bed and slowly crawled in next to her husband. She lay down closely next to him and turned her back to him. Their bottoms touched and she focused on his breathing. He did not snore this time, and when she closed her eyes, sleep came quickly.

~

Besides the obvious issues they had in the bedroom and the doubts she had experienced in the first few weeks, Louise was rapidly getting used to her new day-to-day life with August. Although they were very different, they seemed to complement each other. Louise was realistic and worry-free while August was heavyhearted sometimes and much of a dreamer. She made him laugh a lot more, and he gave her the warmth she needed from time to time. And more importantly he gave her all the freedom she longed for. At first she found freedom in engaging in exciting new ventures. She bought a car and drove to Amsterdam, Antwerp and even Paris once. She was a risky driver, usually speeding and passing other automobiles whenever she had the chance. After a while she grew bored with driving and took up something even more exciting: flying. After the AGA-incident August had never refused his new wife anything. So when she asked him if she could go and get flying lessons, he just nodded his head and authorized a check.
He also introduced her to his neighbour Steven.
Steven was a dentist and had also taken up the hobby of flying. He told her that if she wanted to, Steven could teach her the basics and maybe drive her to the nearest aeroplanes. August himself was not very comfortable with new inventions. He was a more

conservative fellow. He appreciated the speed at which the techniques were evolving, for he had seen his printing business skyrocket after he had invested in new equipment. Proudly he would tell Louise all about his ability to produce at a much greater speed, which meant he could print out many more papers. But inventions like passenger aeroplanes and cars that went faster than 100 km an hour were a complete fright to him. His wife obviously felt quite the opposite and he was all too happy about that. He loved her adventurous spirit and encouraged her in any way he could, except of course by participating.

Steven and Louise got along well from the start. He was a lot looser than August, and she loved the drives together to the airport. They had decided that they would take turns driving, and Steven often teased her about her driving skills.

"You drive like a madman!" he would screech from time to time.

"Fortunately for you I don't drive like a madwoman!" Louise, never shy for an answer, replied, smiling before increasing her speed even more.

Louise and Steven had fun together, but almost like a brother and sister. She loved having a friend again. She used to be up to all kinds of no good with her younger brother Jim. Jim was an artist in every sense of the word. He was a graphic designer and had moved to

Amsterdam as soon as he was 18 years old. She missed him ever so much. Compared to him she was conservative and stern. He often drove her mad, but ever since he had moved away she'd missed him intensely. Steven reminded her a little of her brother and she loved him for it. Purely as a friend. She was still madly in love with her husband and loved him for trusting her. He understood, unlike so many other men, that women could be friends with men. August was very modern when it came to matters like these, and never made her feel like he possessed her. So when Steven accidentally stroked her hand at one of the dinners Louise threw with August, she was shocked to the core to feel her entire body shiver.

~

The matter of the bedroom was never really resolved between Louise and August. After that night in the hotel room they had had obligatory sex twice during their honeymoon, and afterwards they unconsciously decided upon once a month on a Saturday. Of course Louise could not live with this arrangement, and she grew discontent with their sex life more and more. Although her love for August had grown during the first months of their marriage, she longed to be touched. And that is just what Steven did at the dinner while the rest of the party was admiring some new painting August had bought. Her body had responded in the way in which a thirsty man responds to water. She could hardly withhold herself from kissing him right there on the spot. She searched for the last bit of strength in her body and waited for everyone to leave the room. She stood up straight and walked past Steven while brushing her arm against his side. Looking over her shoulder, she smiled and winked. She had become increasingly aware of the power of body language ever since she had seduced her Latin teacher, when she was only 16 years old. Steven, doubting his own eyes right now, responded with an eager nod. He followed her but realised soon afterward that she had led him to the dining room, where everyone was having drinks and hors d'oeuvres. He stared at her blankly, and she smiled back and walked on to the kitchen. He followed without thinking and realised what he had done when she started giggling loudly.

"Steven what are you doing in my kitchen? Taking up some cooking classes as well are you?"

He turned his back to walk to the dining room, somewhat embarrassed, when she gently grabbed his hand and whispered:

"Meet me tonight at the Saint John's."

The night went on for an excruciatingly long time according to Louise's watch. She was distracted by her own thoughts constantly. She fought herself almost out loud. She was not used to fighting her own thoughts. Usually her mind, body and soul were in agreement, but now they were quarrelling like jealous sisters. Her body screamed in longing for pleasure, and her mind and soul tried to stop her from shattering her marriage vows. In her heart of hearts she really could not hurt August; he trusted her blindly. She almost cried out loud when she thought of him finding out. The pain he would feel. No, she decided she would not go through with this mad idea of cheating on the man who loved her to such an extent. She simply could not.

CHAPTER FOUR

But she simply did. At some point her body won all the arguments and took over.

She put up a loving face after dinner and started cleaning up the plates when everyone had left.

"Why don't you just leave everything for Martha? She will clean up tomorrow."

"Oh August, I have eaten so much, I must do the dishes to get some exercise. Don't you worry about me my love. Just go to bed."

She was incredibly nervous. Not of him finding out what she was up to. He was too much of a trustful person to think that badly of her, and that made her cry for him even more. She was just nervous of what this decision would mean for the rest of her life. She knew that there would be no turning back if she were to go through with her infidelity tonight. She knew she would keep on living her life in sin if she would not be able to stop herself.

"Well, if that is what you want. It might be for the best, I think that last glass of wine was a bit too much for me to handle."

In fact August had had a lot to drink. Louise knew he would be sleeping in a matter of seconds. Though he did consume a lot of alcohol at social gatherings, she never minded his drinking habits. He kept on being his kind and loving self. The only thing she did not like about his drinking was his snoring afterwards. But this time, she would not mind. In fact she was glad he would most definitely be out cold in a moment's time. Because she would not be able to live with herself if he found out what she was up to tonight.

~

Steven was already at Saint John's when she arrived. He had prepared well for the encounter, which was somewhat peculiar given the amount of time he had had after dinner. He had brought with him a flashlight, blanket and a bottle of wine with two glasses, which he pulled proudly out of his canvas bag. Louise flinched.
"What did you bring all that for," she asked dryly.
"I thought we might as well make it a memorable night."
"I'd rather not if you don't mind, I am not exactly proud of what I am about to do."
She fiddled her fingers nervously. She could still run. Steven's idea of making this a romantic encounter almost made her sick to her stomach. She did not want her head to get involved, let alone her heart.
"So you do want to go through with it? I was hoping you would. I felt something between us the first day we flew together."
Louise decided not to argue. Like most men, Steven was incredibly pleased with himself. And any kind of attention to him was the confirmation he needed to tell himself every woman was dying to be his. In other circumstances Louise would have not let this opportunity slide to call him out on his arrogance. But not tonight. She was tired and emotional, and for some reason just wanted to get it over with.

So she decided to go along with the "first flight" story and focused on the traits she did fancy. His strong arms, quirky smile and rough beard for starters. Physically he was a very attractive man, but he was half the man August was.

August.

She should not be thinking of him right now. It hurt every time she heard his name or saw his face in front of her. For a moment she wanted to turn around and run away, but she felt that if she would not go through with this, she would gradually lose her mind. Every stranger who had grabbed her hand the last couple of weeks had sent an electric shock through her longing body. She was more sexually charged than ever, and something needed to be done.

"Let's go in," she said with no emotion.

"In the church? Are you comfortable committing adultery under the eyes of God?"

"The eyes of God are everywhere, Steven. You do not need to be in a church for that."

But she wasn't too happy about the location either, so when Steven suggested they go to his empty parents' house, she was ever so eager to come along. When they entered the doorway, Steven turned on the light. The bright lamp shone a light to her ever-growing doubts. She looked at Steven, and worried if August would ever find out what she was about to do. When Steven suggested they open a bottle of wine, she grabbed his collar tightly and kissed him in the middle of the hallway. She jumped when he had accidentally let go of his bag and the contents of it smashed onto the floor. He told her to ignore it, picked her up, and took her to the bedroom. He laid her gently onto the bed and she locked her legs around him. He had no other choice but to fall on top of her. His firm body on hers made her at ease, and slowly her body took over. She ripped off his shirt and giggled when she saw his face. She was in charge of the situation again and threw him onto the bed. With a swift movement she took off her dress and bra, and stood before him in nothing but her red panties. He gazed at her and moved forward to grab her middle. She stepped back and pushed him onto the bed once more.

"Stay right where you are."

She removed her panties and let her hair down. Slowly she crawled towards him and removed his trousers. Then she kissed him passionately and bit his lip.

"Can I touch you, Louise?"

She smiled. Yet again she had a man exactly where she wanted him. She shook her head and pulled his hands above his head and started kissing his chest. When she felt him pulsating underneath her, she let go of his hands.

"You can take over now."
Steven eagerly obliged and went to great lengths to please her. Louise closed her eyes and felt the electrifying waves rush through her. For a moment she did not belong to anybody. It was just she, her body and Steven.
After they had smashed her wedding vows in a thousand pieces, Louise got dressed, pulled her hair back again and breathed heavily. She stood straight and turned her face from Steven, who was gazing at her intensely. She breathed in deeply one more time and tried to find her voice.
"I'll be going home now."
"You don't want to stay for a nightcap?"
"I think I have had enough to sleep on as it is, I am afraid."
"I understand. When will I see you again?"
"Next Saturday. When we have flying lessons."
"Yes, but when am I going to see you again, like this?"
"Oh. I don't know to be honest. I will have to think about it."
"You seemed to enjoy it."
"A part of me did."
Louise turned away and ignored his lips that were ready for a goodbye kiss. She rushed downstairs and closed the front door behind her. When she felt the heavy

door fall against her back, she felt like reality had hit her again. Slowly thick tears appeared at the corners of her eyes, and before she knew it she fell down onto the doorsteps. There were no thoughts or regrets that filled her mind. Only tears. She picked herself up after what felt like hours, and walked back to her townhouse a few meters down the road. She could hear his snoring as soon as she opened the door, and had to hold back another stream of tears. She blew her nose, went to the bathroom and got ready for bed. When she looked in the mirror she saw a different woman from the one who had done her make-up just a few hours ago. She turned down the light and crawled next to August into their bed.

CHAPTER FIVE

Louise could not remember when she had left these intense feelings of guilt behind her. Cheating on August had become second nature for her, and for a short while she had convinced herself that this way both August and she would be happier. It was not until she found out she was expecting, that the guilt came rushing back. All of a sudden the weight of her actions pressed upon her because she was almost sure this baby would not be August's. They still had their Saturday morning sessions every so often, but those sessions had slipped from a monthly to a very sporadic affair. It would be nothing short of a miracle if this baby would indeed share his genes. She decided not to tell August about her pregnancy until the doctor had told her more about when she had conceived the child. As she walked to the doctor's office she thought back to the day she might have gotten pregnant. It should have been a while ago. Morning sickness had already started. Normally that should have alarmed August, but luckily August was a very busy man and had not noticed anything different about her. Besides, she had developed terrible headaches during their short marriage, and those headaches were often paired with nausea. He would not know the difference yet, but she had to tell him soon for her stomach was slowly growing.

Her doctor's office was just a few streets down the road from their marital home. She would usually go by car, simply because she had the option, but today she preferred to walk. Louise did not ponder about many things in life. She usually had to say things out loud before she knew how she felt about them. The only time she did take the time to think was when she was walking through the little town centre of Roosendaal. She would aimlessly stroll around the townhouses and tiny shops for an hour or so, and afterwards her head would feel empty and clean. She had hoped the walk to her doctor's would have the same effect. Unfortunately she felt more panicked when she arrived than she did before. She went into the villa where the GP held his practise, and she sat down to wait for her turn. She fiddled with her hands and looked desperately at the clock. When he opened the door, she took a deep breath and went in.
"Congratulations, Louise. You are indeed with child. Have you told August yet?"
"No doctor, I have not. I wanted to be absolutely sure. I think he would be over the moon with this news and I did not want to get his hopes up for nothing."
"How far along am I?"
She looked at her new doctor nervously and wondered if he could feel her uncertainty about the father of the

child. This man had known August's family forever, and would not be pleased if he found out the new wife of his beloved patient August had gone and made a baby with another man.

"When did you have your last period?"

Louise remembered well. She had never had a regular period, so it had always come as a sort of a surprise. She remembered she was having her flow when spring had first shown its face, which was – if she remembered correctly – in early February. She had been flying all day long and had enjoyed the cloudless sky. Afterwards Steven and she had gone for a walk and ended up making love in the bushes not far from the aeroplane. When they were finished he had asked her if he had hurt her in any way, for there was blood everywhere. She was quite embarrassed about it and just hurriedly whispered she had just started her period.

"The first week of February if I remember correctly?" she finally answered.

"That sounds about right, I can already hear the heart beating. That would mean you are around 15 weeks pregnant. Give or take a week or so."

Louise was frantically thinking if she and August had made love around that time, and could not remember well. She just had to take her chances. She knew he would be so happy if they could celebrate their love with a baby of their own.

"Thank you, doctor. I will go and tell August now. I am sure he will be thrilled!"

She was sure. As long as he was not suspicious, everything would be all right. Louise's guilt grew with every step. She could not enjoy this pregnancy one little bit until she was certain that August was all right. She was not sure what she feared most: the possibility of breaking up their marriage or hurting someone she loved, and who trusted her so wholeheartedly. And what if he was not suspicious yet, but the child grew up to be black-haired and brown-eyed?

She did not think of Steven once. He was the last thing on her mind right now. She was still lost in her thoughts when she almost walked past their home. She felt the nausea rising up again when suddenly she realised August would not be home yet. His days at the office kept on extending, and lately he had not come home before 7 pm. She had complained about these hours to him a couple of times. Simply because she loved having dinner with him and discussing the day with him. To her, August was her companion and true partner, for he understood her like no other. And she loved it when he brought out his red wine after dinner and started to comment on the radio. He knew so much about current events. And there was a lot going on at that time. The economical crisis was at its high point and Hitler's ideas became more radical every day. Because of August's knowledge he was able to provide her with much more information than the presenters on the radio. She truly missed those nights more and more.

But now she was happy that she would not have to face him any time soon. It gave her more time to think. Think about how she would break the news to August. She needed it to be a happy message. But happy was the one emotion she was not feeling at the moment. So how would she ever bring him the news with a smile? One of her migraines was bound to break through.

Luckily Martha was busy cooking up a roast, and Louise loved helping her in the kitchen. Her friends found it extremely odd that she helped the maid. They would blame her background for it. Tilburg was known to be much more liberal. It was an industrial city where people of different classes lived alongside each other. But that is not why she loved cooking with Martha. She actually enjoyed her company and found her stories about her former home in Germany ever so interesting. She also liked her cooking skills. She could whisk an egg with a delicate twist of her wrist. Something Louise had tried to do as well, but instead she had clumsily dropped the bowl onto the floor. Martha had laughed until she cried.

"Oh Martha, I am so happy to see you. I could really

use advice from a friend." Louise grabbed the onions from the kitchen counter and started dicing them.

Her friends thought it strange she referred to some of her maids as friends, too. They never did speak to their maids, which Louise thought to be peculiar. After all, they did all share the same roof.

"What is the matter then, madam? Are you ill still?"

"On the contrary, Martha. On the contrary. I am with child!"

When she said it out loud she felt happy for just a moment. It was as if she had not realised she would become a mother. A tear appeared at the corner of her eye, and she quickly wiped it away before looking at Martha. It could easily have been a tear from dicing the onions. Martha just stared at her with her knife still in her hand, and for a brief moment Louise feared that she had known all along. She loved August like a brother, Louise then thought. Later on she would see the love Martha had for August somewhat less fraternally. The friendly bond Louise and Martha shared in the early days sadly changed throughout the years. At one point they would both fail to understand each other on every single level. The way they interacted those first years seemed long gone after Louise fell deeper and deeper into her betrayal, and more out of love with August.

But Martha put down her knife slowly, breathed in and

started screaming like a pig that is finally presented with its dinner. Louise burst out laughing, for it was a hilarious sight. Martha ran up to her and gently hugged Louise, grabbed her shoulders and looked her right in the eyes, a gaze Louise found difficult. Would Martha be able to see the mixed feelings she was experiencing right now? But Martha just kissed her and started talking to her stomach. Louise sighed and finally allowed herself to be happy with the bundle of joy that was growing in her.

When August came home Louise was at ease. Martha's sincere reaction had taken away most of her fears, but when she saw August's loyal face appear at the window she cringed. She realized she must get it over with before he might suspect something. As always, he would first hang his coat and hat and almost run towards Louise to greet her. After they would share the initial news of the day, he would retire to the study to pour himself a fine whisky. She knew not to bother him before his ritual was finished. His business had increased its turnover, which was nothing short of a miracle in the time of the big depression. Although both Louise and August were very happy with the progress the business was making, it did mean that August was busier than ever. Louise often found him working after hours and feared he would not be able to work at such a pace for a long time.

"Hello, my love, how has your day been today? Have you been feeling better?"
Louise went up to her husband and kissed his forehead. It was always quite clammy and salty, but she had really come to love the sensation on her lips. It truly tasted of her husband.
"Well actually, I went to the doctor's today."
She took a deep breath but was interrupted before she could say anything else.
"O Louise darling. Go and sit down."
"MARTHA!" he yelled. "Can you bring my wife some soup or fruit, she is not feeling well!"
"No, no August." Louise laughed. "I am not sick you fool! I am having your baby!"
She did not know why she had put it so explicitly. She just really wanted it to be true. This man who loved her so purely would be the best father she could ever imagine for her future children. August was still looking at her with his mouth and eyes wide open. He searched for a chair and when Martha came into the room with some grapes, the poor woman had to throw away anything she held in her hand to be able to grab him before he tumbled over her.
"We are having a baby?" was his silent reply.
Louise looked hard for a trace of doubt or anger but could not really discover any emotion. August just kept

on staring until his eyes had filled up with moistness. She was not sure if it was tears or just his eyes protesting exposure to so much oxygen. Louise clapped her hands in front of his face. Slowly August grabbed her hands and brought them to his cheeks and squeezed them. He closed his mouth and swallowed.
"I don't think anyone will ever make me happier than you make me, my love."
He kissed her lips, grabbed her by the waist and threw her upon his lap before he realized she was indeed pregnant, and started apologizing a thousand times.
"It's all right, darling, honestly. I am already 15 weeks on my way and its heart is beating steadily, according to the doctor."
August kissed her stomach and looked up to her.
"You can truly do anything you set your mind to. You are an amazing woman, Marie Louise. "

CHAPTER SIX

When Gus was born Louise did not want to see anyone for over a month. Christmas came and went, but she could not get out of bed. She could not figure out why she was so tired all the time. The labour had been exhausting of course, but she had not heard of other mothers struggling afterwards to even pick up a towel. Most of them just got happier and more energetic. Louise could not even go to the bathroom for a good bath for an entire month. It felt like cotton balls had gotten stuck in her brains, and as if her limbs were made of dough. Not even the angelic face of Gus could lift her spirits. In fact it made her feel wearier altogether. It was not as though she did not love this little creature she had made. She felt very protective of the little man in her arms. But keeping a thought in her head that lasted for over a minute was impossible. And that made it very hard to take care of her son.

For weeks she could not get up to get dressed to get downstairs to see her beloved father-in-law, and after the birth she had let her parents, brother and sister visit her bedroom. She slept for hours and when she was awake she often did little more than stare at the wall of her bedroom. She did try some reading. August had made sure the new Daphne du Maurier, an author she had loved from The Loving Spirit, was ordered in from England especially for her. But even her novel Julius could not keep her focused.

August was worried sick but let her be. They were only married for a year and a half, but he knew that whenever she was tired or suffered from a migraine, he could best leave her alone. It was a different situation now with her being a first-time mother, and he was worried that motherhood scared her. He went to great lengths to try and find out more about the subject. He talked to the doctor about Louise's condition, but he advised August to just let her rest. He needed to bring Gus to her whenever he needed to eat, to stimulate the bonding with his mother. But August did not think the problem lay there. Louise looked ecstatic whenever she laid her eyes on little Gus. She would stroke his little head for hours on end until he dozed off into a deep sleep. August felt that it might have something to do with the newfound responsibility Louise had gained. He knew that above all Louise liked to be free. She did not want to be pinned down at all. He had never minded giving her the freedom she so desperately desired. But with Gus' arrival he guessed that Louise felt her days of freedom were over. She was still relatively young, 23, and although many women of her age had multiple children, Louise still was rather carefree. Little did he know that Louise's sickness had not much to do with the responsibility that came with being a mother. Of course she realized that her carefree days were behind her, but that was something she was happy to sacrifice for little Gus. It was the guilt she felt that had left her feeling empty and tired. Seeing Gus made her doubt no more about who the father was. She had hoped for a long time that God would have been kind and let August be the father of her firstborn, but Gus' features left little to the imagination. This was Steven's child.

Steven of course had known his neighbour and mistress was expecting a child, and did wonder a lot about who the father might be. He knew that he probably was the father, but Louise had refused to speak to him ever since she had found out she was pregnant. He had begged and had written her letters, which he had found back ripped or partly burned on his doorstep. She wanted nothing to do with him, as if she could have changed the genes of this child by ignoring his existence. Steven had let it go for a while, for he was about to be married to his long-time girlfriend. He had left Louise alone and had gotten no invitations for any other dinner parties at her house. He was fine with the situation until Gus was born. He did find it a bit overdramatic to name the child who obviously was not August's, after August. It had struck him that Louise could have just erased him from her life.

Louise might have had erased Steven out of her life,

but with little Gus staring at her she knew once and for all that Steven would never be gone from her life entirely. In fact, he would stay with her for the rest of her life whether she wanted him to or not. That very thought had made her into the tired mess that she was at the moment. She could not even find the strength to come up with a way to get herself together for August.

When the holidays were over and everyone had returned to their normal lives, Louise started to get better gradually. She started off with bathing herself and getting dressed. After a while she was able to go to church on Sundays, and come February she was finding herself in a state she almost recognised from before she gave birth.

Gus made up for the pain she was feeling from her betrayal. He seemed to be a happy child, not too damaged from her post-labour illness, as she would later call it. August loved everything about Gus and cared for him in a way fathers of that time usually did not. He fed the little boy and even changed his nappies once. Louise thoroughly enjoyed his fatherly love, but bitterly wondered if she enjoyed it so much because it meant that August did not have a clue that this child did not share his genes. She wished she could savour the blessings of her family, but she struggled to. She was convinced this was her punishment.

In the beginning of spring Louise felt herself

becoming her old self again. With the return of her old self, her old urges came back as well. During her pregnancy and so-called labour illness, she was reluctant to think of any sort of intimacy, but as soon as she had felt her old self come back to life, so did her desires to be a woman. And after giving birth it seemed as though August was even more frightened to look at her as something other than a mother. At the end of February when it was still cold, she crawled next to him like she always did, but this time she had failed to put on her nightgown. She curled her legs around his waist and gently caressed his chest hair. He turned to her immediately when he felt her lack of panties, and pushed her legs away from his waist.

"Should we be making love already Louise? Are you healed yet?"

Louise sighed and swallowed back some tears.

"I gave birth three months ago, August; I am sure I will be fine. Some other mothers have already conceived their next child after three months."

She turned away from him and lay on her side. She could not hide her disappointment, for she knew that their nightly life would never get better, it would only get worse.

"Well, let us just wait until little Gus is a bit older. He might hear us and I am not sure if that is advisable."

Louise got out of bed and ignored August's apologies.

She put on her underwear and night gown and went downstairs for a night cap. She sat in his chair and stared out the window. How on earth was she supposed to make this marriage and family a happy one, when they would not be able to live as a true husband and wife? She could not talk to August about her feelings, for it would now be too late. She had already conceived their child with another man and there was no way she could express her discontent after a year of deceiving him. She felt she had to find a way to make them both happy. And that meant that she would always have to have a man on the side, even though it was never the way she had thought of her marriage beforehand. She was not as romantic as he was, but she certainly had not imagined her life to be so complicated and bitter so soon after saying "I do." She felt sorry for herself for the first time since she had gotten married to August. Ever since that first night she had spent with Steven, she had felt guilty about what she was doing. But now she felt that August was to blame for this situation as well. What did he expect? The one thing that separated a marriage from a friendship was intimacy. It was as vital to a marriage as love, she thought. Of course she knew the stories of people getting married for status or money or opportunities, but it had never been her idea to marry for those reasons. And she was sure it was not August's idea either. Call her naïve or a hopeless romantic, she had married August for love and companionship, and she had always expected she would be happy with just him forever.

She had never felt alone before in her life, but now in her marital home, she did. She knew all too well that from now on this would not be a happy marriage. Someone was bound to get hurt. And at this point this person was Louise. She became less concerned about August's feelings, for she felt he should have known by now he was not fulfilling his wedding vows. From this night on, Louise's and August's happy marriage changed for good.

CHAPTER SEVEN

John was quite different from her former lovers. Usually she would fall for the kind and gentle sort of men, but she was not in the market for a companion, she wanted a true lover. And John had all the traits of a good one. He was handsome in a more obvious way and knew how to get on with the ladies. He was a popular fellow and quite known for his exploits. Louise was not impressed by his popularity. But she was intrigued by his adventures. Her friend Cissy had introduced John to her a year after she had given birth to Gus, when Louise was desperate for a man.
Cissy turned out to be a real gem in a sea of mud when it came to friends in Roosendaal. Louise had never before had trouble befriending girls. Ever since she was a little girl she found it easy to make friends with both boys and girls. And once a friendship was made, it was usually a bond that would turn out to last a lifetime. She would still write with some of the girls she had met at boarding school. Heck, she even wrote letters to Fons' wife. Correspondence she began to cherish more and more. But in Roosendaal it had been increasingly different for Louise to make any friends. Of course she had tried. August and she had thrown numerous parties for mainly his friends, but their wives had found her strange and way too forward. They would laugh at her

jokes and politely ask after her health, but Louise knew all too well that they weren't at all sincere. But Cissy was a welcome exception to the rule. She found Louise thrilling and smart as opposed to overdramatic and a show-off. So Cissy and Louise clung on to each other more and more since Louise's life had been more bound to Roosendaal.

Of course Cissy officially did not know anything of Louise's betrayal, but she did suspect that Louise did not behave as well as she would have liked her to believe. She had never expected to set her up with a lover though.

They met at the opening of a new book store. At first she did not like his boyish looks and Casanova-like manners at all. But when he had started telling her about his flights to Indonesia and encounters with the wonderful nature and wildlife there, she started to feel herself warming up to this confident man. She was very eager to fly such a distance herself, and could herself not wait to visit other countries. The fact that he was interested in those kinds of adventures made up for his openly flirting with every lady on offer. She did not feel any competition though, for she thought herself to be much more attractive than any other woman in Roosendaal. Of course there were more beautiful and slimmer girls, but she, she felt, had unique views of the world and had so much more to offer.

"So I have heard that you have seen quite some exotic places lately?"
Immediately she noticed she liked him more than she had expected to. Usually she would not open with such an obvious flattery. Of course, she was just stating a fact, but most men she knew would instantly take a harmless remark like this one as a compliment. It did not make her bitter, she kind of loved men for their confidence and the fact that they got away with it.
"I wonder where you got that information, madam. This town rarely talks."
His witty reply surprised her. It instantly made him much more interesting than she had suspected when first laying eyes on him. His remark was right up her alley, for she herself had been the subject of the town's talks on more than one occasion. He must have heard some of those stories too, given his answer.
"So what else have you been doing besides educating the local authorities?"
She wanted to let him know she had heard about him too. Cissy had told her John had gone to Indonesia to prepare the country for an independent political position in the Dutch commonwealth. Something that had impressed Louise, for it had been a new and liberal view in that time. That still did not warm her up to him though; until his witty remark she had found him thick-

headed and arrogant.

He did not bat an eyelid when he found out she knew this about him. He must have blamed gossip, or women, or the fact that no one could help but to talk about him.

"Enjoying the country first and foremost. It is completely different from the world we are familiar with, and I would love to live there one day."

"That would be such a shame. Whom should I be talking to on these boring gatherings when someone like you is not around to entertain me?"

He chuckled loudly and almost spilled his drink on her off-white dress. When he had refreshed their drinks and straightened his jacket he cheekily replied.

"Shall I brighten up your next party too then?

She did not want to be one of his many, but after a while she gave into his charms and invited him over for one of her dinner parties. She did not feel guilty inviting over potential lovers. In fact, she rarely felt guilty about anything anymore. She had now convinced herself that August had singlehandedly sabotaged their marriage by not giving her the sexual fulfilment she so longed for. And besides, he was oblivious to her intentions. In fact, it turned out that August started to like John a lot. Mainly because of their differences. It was an unfortunate trait of his to truly love people who could not be tamed. Like Louise, John was kind of a

daredevil and knew how to entertain August for nights in a row. Mainly with his stories about Indonesia, his rides on elephants and dives with sharks. August could not get enough of John's adventures, and neither could Louise.
Besides the ability to get her full attention with his stories, he had a talent that turned out to get to her even more. He was the best lover she had been with yet, and she grabbed every opportunity she got to take off his clothes.
She had gotten less careful because of it, and the town could not get enough of the gossip their affair provided. Louise knew this all too well, but it did not bother her much. A part of her actually wanted August to find out so that he would see what his actions, or rather, his lack of actions had led to. But of course she knew he would never look at their situation that way. He would feel betrayed beyond belief. Another part of her wanted to keep their marriage alive, and that part had won the internal fight she held regularly, still. In order to stay in this relationship somewhat wholeheartedly, she knew she had to keep on making love to her husband, even if they both did not seem to get much joy out of it. But she had to be on the safe side in case she would become pregnant again; she had learned that much ever since the expected arrival of Gus.

Louise, always interested in novel inventions and methods, had read about a new way of contraception invented by a Dutch gynaecologist. It was based on the regularity of the woman's cycle, and all she had to do was count the days after her menstruation. She had embraced the Rhythm method directly after Gus was born, and it had not let her down yet. But because of her irregular periods she knew she had to be careful still. Although she grew unhappy with her marriage every day, she did not want to lose August, and she was sure she would not get away with bearing another child out of wedlock.

August was not aware of his wife's affairs. He focused on his ever-growing printing business and the charity work he had also taken on. Although he was not as charming as his father, he was as much of a people person and with everything that was happening in the world, he felt there was no other option for him than to use his position for the good of society. Together with his work as a director, it meant that he was very rarely at home. And when he was at home, he and Louise usually had people over. They were at their best in the company of others. He loved seeing her entertain their friends, and she glowed with pride whenever he started sharing his views on the world.

She still thought him to be the smartest and most considerate man she knew. She herself was very much involved in his charity work as well, and helped him whenever she could. As long as they were working or entertaining together, they were the perfect couple. But as soon as their guests had closed the door, the couple usually was lost for words. He would drunkenly stumble into his bed while she would often sneak out of the house to visit John.

John lived on his own a minute's bike ride away, so it did not take Louise much effort to pay him a visit every so often. On nights when they would come together, he would leave his door unlocked. She would often find him reading in his chair with the drapes drawn. Before entering the room she'd make sure to take off her shoes and sneak upon him, close his book for him, and finally lean in for a kiss. The very repetition of their encounters was something she had rapidly come to dislike, for she was bored easily. But it was tiring coming up with new ways for their rendezvous, for they had to be careful to not fuel the rumour mill even more. He had found someone he wanted to marry as well, and although he was not inclined to give up Louise just yet, he did not want to hurt his bride to be.

"Let's go upstairs," she whispered while she closed his book.

"Wait Louise, just let me finish this chapter."

She scowled. Their affair had begun to look like a marriage more and more.

"No I will not wait, for I have waited long enough. Come upstairs with me or I will leave."

"Leave if you will, my love, you can try to persuade your snoring husband to entertain you I suppose."

She felt offended. Although she had told John about August and her problems, he was not the one to judge him.

"Maybe you should reconsider your fiancée as well then, as she is so obviously lacking any skills to keep you to herself."

It was a bitter response. It was unlike Louise, who was usually charming even when she felt offended.

"You really are in a foul mood, Louise. What is the matter?" he asked with true concern.

John really meant well, she supposed. He had become an unlikely friend as well as her lover.

"Oh I don't know, really. I feel like I am stuck in a rut and I can't get out of it. My marriage is not working out the way I had imagined it to, this town is getting on my nerves, and motherhood is really tiring to be honest."

Little Gus was a happy baby, but also a very demanding one. He had grown into a very loud three-year-old, and that day she was not even able to hold a conversation

of more than a minute before he would start to fiddle with the piano. He would crawl onto the chair and often risk his little life to push his fingers onto the keys. It was just plain noise he produced, but for some reason he kept on trying to play. Louise had cared for him the entire day, for Martha was in Germany with her family, and August obviously was much too busy to help her out. At night they had had guests over, and without Martha she had to do most of the cooking herself, for she would not have one of the other maids working in her kitchen. She felt exhausted and longed for bed. But her body had been yearning for her night with John all day, and she knew better than to ignore it.
"Let's just go upstairs."
John obeyed, for there was no way he would be able to finish his chapter with her being all gloomy. He tried to lift her spirits by picking her up and carrying her off to his bed. She did cry out loud and giggled all the way up. "That's better." he said with a smile, and threw her jokingly onto his bed.
He tried to undress her but he knew she would never let him take charge. He was surprised to find she did let him undo her dress, and he eagerly went on with stroking her soft skin.
"What is the matter, Louise? You never leave me in charge."
"Let's not talk about it, Johnny. I just want to fight off

the noise in my head, and you are the only one with the powers to do so. Just lead me into ecstasy."

And so he did. He gently pulled her up and kissed her from her neck down. He lifted up her arms and lovingly kissed her lips. While holding her wrists in one hand he kept on stroking her skin with the other. He proceeded to squeeze her curvy hips and laid his head on her soft stomach. Unable to withhold herself, she lifted her head, freed her wrists and folded herself onto him. They lay like that for a while, then she let go and went to lie on her side. She looked at him and wondered when exactly she had started to love him. When she was looking into his dark eyes she realized for the first time that she was not only seeing him for the physical attraction. She really felt at ease whenever she was close to John. She felt tears sting in the back of her eyes, and decided to turn her back to him before he would see her cry. She turned around slowly while he wrapped himself around her. It was this night that they would conceive their child.

CHAPTER EIGHT

Betty was born two weeks before Gus' fourth birthday. She looked much like her little brother as a baby. Both Steven and John were dark-haired, and so were their children. This time Louise was not nearly as tired as she was after giving birth to Gus. It was a different feeling altogether, mainly because she was happier this time. This child was born out of love. And although she would be raised by a different father, Louise would not keep her from her real one. Luckily August did not suspect anything, and proudly introduced his little baby girl to John. Louise was surprised to find August so happy. She had not paid much attention to him during her pregnancy, and did not know he was so happy with another child. He and Betty were inseparable from day one. Often she would find him and Gus hovering over Betty's crib, and for a brief moment she felt happy again with her family. She had found a way to be as happy as possible in a not-so-happy marriage, but if she was given the choice she would rather experience a more traditional form of marital bliss. She had never let Steven near Gus, but she had decided not to keep John away from little Betty. John had meant more to Louise than Steven ever had, and she found it vital to Betty's upbringing that she would get to know the man who had given her part of her genes. She knew it was unorthodox, but she prided herself on being a different thinker. She also no longer feared August finding out the truth. It seemed he was immune to all the rumours about Louise. She was not sure whether he ignored all the stories, or people were just too scared to tell him. But in fact no one who knew August would have the guts to shatter his dream marriage. August was a much-loved man in the Roosendaal community, and although they were protective of him and sometimes hated Louise for her betrayal, they knew all too well that August would never survive the blow of her infidelity. The best thing to do was to not tell him, the town mutually agreed. And besides, they liked the gossip Louise and John provided. There was no better entertainment around. Not even the plays in the theatre August was responsible for.

After Betty was born, John and Louise felt their love deepen for each other – which made things more complicated. John, being married now, no longer lived on his own and could not meet up with Louise in his home. They had to come up with more creative ways of meeting up. Booking a hotel room was one of them. They would meet during the day rather than at night, for John could not be seen leaving his house after hours without arousing some suspicion. His wife was from out of town, and was also oblivious to all the gossip, but John expected she would hear about it soon, and begged Louise for more discretion. She had grown even more careless after Betty's birth, for reasons unknown to even herself. John and Louise quarrelled about this regularly when they were in the privacy of their hotel room.

"I think we need to stop seeing each other for a while before my wife starts to suspect something, Louise. She is pregnant with my baby."

"So? I have given birth to your baby very recently, as you might recall."

She hated these discussions. It undermined their love, she thought.

"A baby who cannot carry my name, indeed, madam. So I would really like it that the next baby I have conceived would in fact carry my name if you do not mind."

John sighed and looked at his mistress. Their affair had lasted for over three years, and he had really grown to love her. But he did find her insufferable when it came to the subject of his wife. For some reason she felt entitled to a husband but at the same time she was very resentful about him having a wife. She was incredibly charming towards Susanne whenever she would see her, and his wife absolutely adored her. But he doubted whether Louise would stop her car if she were to find his wife lying on the road in front of it.

"Louise, this situation is becoming ridiculous and I need it to stop. I can barely sleep at night."

"Oh you poor thing. It is hard entertaining two gorgeous women, I understand. Let me not stand in your way."

She grabbed her bag and tried to hold back the tears she felt prickling in the back of her eyes. She did not want him to see her cry. Before she had time to leave the hotel room, he grabbed her by the arm.

"Don't go, darling," he whispered in her ear.

"We have been through so much together, I do not want to see us part like this."

"But you do want to part with me! You do want to put an end to all we have together."

Louise did not know why she had to sound so dramatic. Perhaps because she could not bear to live her life without him. John turned her towards him and took her face in between his large hands. He looked into her eyes and wondered how those innocent eyes could belong to such an experienced and powerful woman. He had never met anyone like her, and this was the first time he had ever seen her fragile side. It softened him to see her in such a state. He planted a kiss on her lips, which were salty and moist, a sign she had been crying.

"Let's not quarrel, Louise. Let's just go to bed."

For once Louise was not in the mood. She would rather lie in his arms for hours on end. But she knew that the one thing that kept them together was their mutual longing for physical pleasures, so she went along with his wishes.

After that time Louise and John rarely met up. They saw each other when one of their spouses threw a dinner party, and even then they would not so much as exchange a mutual joke. Louise did, however, make sure that John would not miss much of Betty. Whenever he and Susanne came around, she took little Betty downstairs and talked all about how she had grown, and about whether she was teething or crawling yet. John's wife had given birth to a baby boy and was very interested in little Betty's progression. It gave Louise carte blanche to inform John fully about his daughter. She would let him hold her regularly on the pretext of letting him get used to infants. She was, however, heartbroken that their private meetings occurred no longer. He had never given her any explanation for it, but simply never called on her again after that afternoon in their hotel room. There was no way she could reach him, for his wife was always at home. She did not want to write him as she was sure that Susanne would intercept the letter, and if she were to find out about the two of them, chances were that Louise would never see him again. Visiting his work was too desperate a measure for Louise's liking. It was clear to her he had his reasons, and the only way to get him back was to allow him to miss her.

~

Come spring, she asked August if she could visit Fons and his wife Helen. She and Fons had kept in touch throughout the years even though he had moved all the way to The Hague, a two-hour drive from Roosendaal. August and Louise often visited the couple in summer, but this year August could not find the time to join her, so she asked him if she could go by herself instead. It would be nice to get out of town and clear her head for a while. She would ask Fons if she could be joining them at their summer home too, in the middle of the country. She had always liked it there, and she loved the company of both Fons and Helen. August of course said yes. He was happy that she had found a way to spend her summer. She would take Gus and Betty with her so he could concentrate on work and work alone.

Louise decided to drive to Fons herself. She put Gus in the passenger seat with little Betty on top of his lap in her carry basket. He adored his little sister and protected her like she was the most precious thing this world had ever seen. Betty was a silent girl, in contrast to her older brother. She rarely woke up during the night, whereas her brother would still regularly wake up happy to make some excessive noise. Because of the children, she thought it best to stop along the road a couple of times. When she'd just gotten married to August she would drive all the way to Amsterdam without stopping once, but she had children now and she could not just concentrate on the road anymore. She was a strict mother and did not want her children to misbehave, so even when she was driving she was very much paying attention as to what Gus was doing or saying. She wanted to be stricter than her own sweet mother. Her parents had always been too sweet for her and her siblings. Especially for her brother. Although she loved Jim more than any other man, she thought him too much of a free spirit. Sure, she considered herself to be one as well, but all within good reason. If asked, Louise would describe her brother as someone who forgot about reality way too often. She wondered if she would go and visit him while she stayed with Fons. Maybe he could even see the children, for he loved his nephew and she was sure he would love to see his niece again. He had only seen her once after she was born. His graphic designs were keeping him rather busy. He had landed a job with an advertisement bureau and was designing for many commercials. She had seen some of the national advertisements in the papers, and it had filled her with pride. Her little sister had been less successful in life, according to Louise. Sylvie had married a horrible man and had given birth to three children already, and with another one on the way Louise thought her to have become nothing but a breeding machine. Her husband had no civil bone in his body and was horrible to his wife. She often spoke to her brother about this, but they did not see eye to eye about the matter. He said that Sylvie was happy being a mother, and that Hans was a kind man, just not as charming as the men Louise would fall for. Jim knew about the affairs his older sister had from time to time. He was the only one Louise confided in. He lived far away and understood her better than anyone else because he had the same kind of urges as she had. But him being a bachelor in a quite bohemian city, he did not encounter the same difficulties as Louise. That made her envy his life sometimes. Life was so unfair for a woman, according to Louise.

When she arrived at Fons' and Helen's house after a few hours, she was welcomed by their three-year-old daughter.

"Auntie Louise has arrived, daddy! And she has brought Gus with her for me to play with!"

Gus crossed his little arms and stomped his feet.

"I will not be playing with a girl, mama. I simply cannot do such a thing."

Louise laughed at the comments of her son, and replied he would soon be thinking very differently about that matter.

"It seems as though they are made for each other already!" Fons bellowed when he saw little Gus pushing away his daughter.

"Soon she will be pushing him over, by the sight of it. She is a feisty little thing. She must have gotten that from her mother." Louise kissed Fons on the cheek and fiddled with his hair.

"What are you doing with my husband, madam? I believe you have had your chance with him and you decided to rudely dump him for another."

Louise giggled when she heard Helen's voice, and she let go of Fons to give Helen a hug.

"Always a delight to see you, my dear. Oh, and I can see that that foul husband of yours has once again worked his magic."

Approvingly she softly patted the slightly bigger stomach of her normally very slim friend.

"We have the obligation of producing a little boy for Betty, have we not?"

"You certainly have, Helen. You most certainly have."

Fons and Helen were a joy to be with. For the first time since Gus was born she was able to leave her troubles behind her. For once she did not have to think about August or John, or John's wife. She could just enjoy the countless conversations. Fons and Helen had gone out of their way to please her. They knew she loved meeting new people and had invited many fresh faces to their dinners. Finally, after living in Roosendaal for six years, she met people who were not as narrowminded as most of the people she had met there. August was not narrowminded and neither was John, but there were many others who got frightened by the very mention of change. Louise had yearned for change her entire life. Stagnation she found turned out ever to be so boring.

To repay Helen's and Fons' kindness she offered to cook them a great dinner at the end of her stay. They had after all taken care of her for four weeks — at first in their townhouse in The Hague, and later they had taken her to their holiday home in 't Gooi, a posh and green area in the middle of the country. Louise and her children had enjoyed every hour of it, and so Louise decided to thank them in the best way she could; by cooking one of her much-appreciated dinners. Helen had offered to help her in the kitchen and they had a grand old time. The circumstances in which she had met Helen were not exactly ideal, but they had liked each other immediately. Both Fons and Louise had always been relaxed about the annulment of their engagement, and Helen was also to thank for that. Fons had fallen for her when he still was with Louise, and was afraid to break the news to her. Helen had been sure there was no love between Louise and Fons, and had jovially confronted Louise with the matter. Coincidentally, Louise had just met August, and to hear what Helen had to say was, needless to say, much of a

relief. But the fact that Helen had come forth with the situation so bluntly had really made her a friend for life. Louise had loved her right from that moment. That was why, when Helen had asked her during the preparations for the dinner, she was just as honest about the state of her marriage as Helen was back then.
"I have gotten myself into a real pickle, Helen."
She was glad she could talk to someone she trusted other than Jim. The fact that Helen was a woman made talking somewhat easier.
"What have you been up to now, you dirty woman?"
Louise had already told Helen once about Steven. She had never told anyone that Gus was not August's though. But Helen did know she had been unfaithful to August before.
"I have done it again, Helen. But this time I have gotten in over my head. I think I love him."
Helen stopped chopping carrots and stared at her friend.
"Does that mean that you stopped loving August?"
"Oh I don't know. We seem to have grown apart even more. He is always busy, and we hardly ever even speak to each other when no one else is around. I do feel alone most of the time."
When she said it out loud she felt that that was the main problem. In Roosendaal she did not have many friends. Other women, except for Cissy, found her

exotic and were scared to really talk to her. She tried her hardest to befriend them, but nothing had seemed to stick. August never had much time for her, and she could only get his attention when they had visitors. John had listened to her when they were alone, and really savoured the moments they had together.

"Do you think I should give my marriage another chance?"

She knew that if she wanted to keep their marriage a loving one, she had no other choice.

"I think you need to talk to him first and foremost. I am sure he would drop anything if you would ask him to. If he knew you felt that way he would do anything to make you feel better, and you know that."

She did know it. Why it had not occurred to her before, she did not know, but she was determined to work at their marriage once more.

That night she was even merrier than she had been the weeks before. Fons and Helen were the right medicine for her gloomy state. She returned to Roosendaal a new woman.

CHAPTER NINE

After she returned from her holiday at Fons' and Helen's, Louise found herself happy to be home again. Although she had not realised it at the time, she had really missed August while she was away. The moment she had set foot in their home she had longed to see August's friendly smile. She decided that she would sit down and talk to him that very night. Helen was right, August would do anything she would ask of him. And she would not ask him for a lot. She just wanted him home more. Although her marriage was not everything she had wanted it to be, she truly loved the man she had said "I do" to six years prior. He still was an extraordinary, intelligent and kind man and he adored her no less after all those years. He was still the only one who understood her best, she thought.

But he loved her like one would love a wild animal. From a distance. He knew he could never domesticate her. When Louise came to talk to him the night she came back, he was expecting the worst. He had not seen her that happy in years, and he did not expect that her mood had anything to do with him.

"I have been talking to Helen a lot while I stayed with Fons and her."

Louise had poured a fine red wine for her and her husband, and sat herself down on his armrest. She had put her feet up onto his lap and fiddled with his thick blonde hair.

"She advised I should just ask you."

"Ask me what, dear? You know you can have anything you want."

August could not relax just yet. He never knew what was coming when Louise was this kind to him. She could easily work herself into a fuming frenzy in a matter of seconds still.

"I do not want anything I want. I want you, my darling."

"But you have me, Marie Louise. I am all yours."

He loved using her full name. He was the only one who ever did. It said something about the way he cherished her. Exactly the way as she presented herself. He would not for the world change her into someone who would fit into his world. He took her exactly the way she was and would, if necessary, build his world around her.

"But I never get to see you. We only speak to each other when we have visitors. You barely talk to me anymore. Or touch me."

He knew this was a problem. But he did not know why he could not touch her the way she wanted him to. He did find her attractive. Very much so. But as soon as he tried looking at her as a sexual human being, his body would protest. He would feel himself weakened and turned off immediately. But he wondered if she got any joy out of their obligatory physical encounters, for she did not seem to. Maybe she had longed for that second child. They had never really talked about children. Becoming parents had just happened. And August could not find himself a happier man in the whole of Roosendaal for it. His children were his pride and joy.

He was surprised that Louise wanted to see more of him. He had always found himself an extremely lucky man for having found someone that special to want to marry him.

"I am sorry to hear that, sweetheart. I honestly did not know you missed me that much."

"Oh but I do, so very much. I miss our evenings together and our Saturday mornings. I miss our laughs and I miss you holding me through the night. I sometimes even wonder if you still love me."

Louise had gotten very emotional all of a sudden. She had not realised before how much she had missed August. And how much their marriage had changed over the years. She was just as much to blame, maybe even more.

"I love you more than words can say, Marie Louise," August interrupted her thoughts.

Of course she knew this. She guessed he would probably love her too much. But she needed him to act on it. She needed him to cherish and care for her like he used to. She needed him to be her husband again.

"Please spend more time with me, August. Let us be husband and wife again."

She looked him in the eye, put her arms around him and slid onto his lap. After what seemed quite a while, August wrapped his arms around his wife and rocked her back and forth. He breathed in her perfume and kissed her hair. Louise could not remember the last time she had held her husband this firmly. But she was sure she had not ever since she had started her affairs. She felt guilty for sabotaging what they had, and she kissed his forehead after letting go carefully. Her eyes were moist and red, and for once she did not mind for August to see her this way. She had never been comfortable with showing her weaknesses to the world. Not even to her loved ones. Even when she had stayed in bed for months after Gus was born, she made sure she looked presentable. During her worst days she would simply let no one into her room. Not even her servants. She would ask them to put the trays with food and water in front of the door. But somehow she did not mind this time. She wanted him to know she was serious.

"Marie Louise, as long as I am alive my only goal in life will be to make you happy. And if it is as easy as spending more time with you, I am yet again the luckiest fellow on earth."

August was a man of his word, and the next day he appointed an assistant-director, so he could be home earlier and clear his weekends for Louise.
Louise decided she would make no effort to see John again. She loved having August around. For the first time since Gus was born it felt like they were a real family. She enjoyed cooking for her husband and children, and felt like a proper housewife for once. She had never aspired to be one before, but it felt amazing after the complicated few years she had been through. It was nice to enjoy her family for a while and it seemed as though it was exactly what little Gus needed. He had calmed down after a matter of days and slept through the night for the first time of his short little life. Betty had always been a calm and happy baby, and was just as lovable as ever. Louise decided August would be just as good a father to her as he had been to Gus, and she let go of the idea of getting her to know her biological father.
She had not seen John since she had been back, and made sure August would not invite him to one of their dinner parties they still regularly held. To make her marriage a success, Louise needed to focus on August and August alone. Besides, John had shown no interest in her lately. Not even while she was away. At first she was hurt to have been so rudely set aside. But later on

Cissy told her that John's wife Susanne had found out about his infidelity, and had threatened to leave him if he started seeing Louise again. She understood his choice, but found him a coward for it and she did not need a spineless man in her life. At this point August was all she needed. Even in the bedroom things started to pick up. August was in no state to compete with her lovers physically, as he had little experience. But he did try his best and Louise appreciated his effort. It felt less obligatory, and for a moment Louise had been able to let go of reality and just enjoy the intimacy she shared with her husband. For the first time in their six-year marriage life was simple. And good.

CHAPTER TEN

And then the war came. Both August and John were called up for mobilization, which left Louise devastated and alone. It was a frightening time. Although the Netherlands had vowed to be neutral, it had become very clear that Germany would not spare their country this world war. She had been very well-informed and knew that what was coming would change their country, and lives for that matter, forever.

When August received his call for the mobilization, Louise vowed to attend the Holy Mass and receive Holy Communion every day until he came back to her. Although she was a realist, matters like these could only be left to prayer. For God would not take her husband away from her now, surely. After she had given their marriage a wholeheartedly new chance. She had decided to show Him her newfound devotion for August by prayer. To August this was the single most moving effort Louise had ever made. He loved her even more for it.

When August was gone he left a gap too great for Louise to fill on her own. The visits to the church kept her busy, but the rest of her days were filled with staring out the window and listening to the wireless. There were times when Louise did not get dressed until she had to leave for church, and afterwards she would go right back to bed. She left Gus' and Betty's care to

Martha, although her trusting maid was even more frightened for her own family in Germany. The only time Martha and Louise shared some smiles was when the mailman arrived with good news letters. Although the Netherlands was not at war yet, there was danger in the air. And with her renewed feelings for August she could not bear to think of the worst scenario.

Louise had heard that John was called up to prepare the Netherlands for the war too, and that news had made her weak in the knees. She had not thought about John for a while but when she found out he would enter the army after mobilization in case of a war, she became very worried. Her feelings for him had not changed, it seemed. For the first time in her life she did not like her own reflection in the mirror. She was a determined woman and always knew exactly what she wanted. If she set her mind to something, she made it happen. But in this frightful time she was not in control. Her emotions took over and although she kept on praying for August's safe return every single day, she could not get John out of her mind. She resented her own feelings and tried to cast them off. But the more she tried not to think of him, the more often he came to her mind, or dreams. She started to have sensual dreams in which he would bring her to ecstasy. She would wake up moaning loudly almost every morning. With August gone, she had asked Martha to sleep in the house with her, and she wondered if Martha would have heard her. After two months she had had enough and decided there was only one way to solve this. She would have to go to confession.

~

She did not visit her own church for this confession. She did not want her own priest to know all about her affairs. She wanted God to know and she yearned for redemption, so she could start again.
"Forgive me father, for I have sinned."
Louise stared at her lap while she recited the words she had said so many times before. But this time she would come forward with all her sins.
"Go on, child."
"I have not been faithful to my husband, and I have given birth to two children out of wedlock."
She could feel the eyes of the priest burning onto her face, but she kept on staring at her hands, tightly tucked in between her legs. She had never been this straightforward about her infidelity. Not even to herself. Saying it out loud in such a blunt manner made her loathe herself. And she had never loathed herself before. She had always found a way to accept her shortcomings, and she easily forgave her own infidelities. But this time Louise had to face her shortcomings to move on and fix what was left of her marriage.
After Louise had said her Hail Marys she felt a bit better. It was as though she had only realised today she had been unfaithful to the one person who loved her truly. And now that person was not even here to

console her. But maybe it was for the best that August was not at home when Louise came back from church, for she would have confessed everything straightaway. Instead she came home to an empty house, as the children were at the park with Martha. She closed the big front door behind her and started sobbing at once. In the privacy of her home she was finally able to let the tears fall freely. She sat down on the first step of the stairs and stroked the Persian carpet August had shipped in for her. It felt soft and warm, and Louise laid her head on the next step and felt the carpet brush against her moist cheeks. She lay there for a while, trembling with tears until her limbs started to hurt. When she crawled up she had to grab the banisters to not fall down on the tiles. The carpet was all wet from her tears, and she wondered if the salt would affect the fabric at all. She straightened her dress and went upstairs. Her bed looked deserted and empty, and she did not feel like sleeping in it at all. Instead she went to Gus' room and got into his bed. Of course she did not fit into the tiny bed, but she pulled her knees to her chin and hugged her shins until she fell asleep.
"Mama, what are you doing in my bed?"
Louise slowly opened her eyes and felt every part of her body cringe in pain. She looked at her handsome son and suddenly realised where she was. She tried to laugh.

"Oh silly mama. I was cleaning up your room and got really tired. Your bed looked so comfortable, Gussie, so I decided to lie down in it for a while."

"I would rather not have you in my bed anymore, mama," Gus said with a stern face. "But this time I don't mind."

Louise laughed a heartfelt laugh this time, and pulled Gus against her chest. She hugged him and kissed his forehead. Gus wrapped his little arms around his mother and kissed her too.

"I do love you, mama, but I love my bed as well."

"I understand, darling. I will never sleep in your bed ever again. I promise."

Gus had brightened up her day a little, and Louise did not think of her confession again until the children were to bed and Martha had gone upstairs to do some sewing. The house felt empty again and apart from the light next to the wireless, Louise sat in the dark. She never noticed the dark. Other people had to turn on the light for her before she would notice that the sun had set. She turned on the wireless to keep her company. The news was not comforting. Germany had invaded Poland and the war everyone feared had officially begun.

But Louise did not think too much about the war that night. Even the invasion of Poland could not stop her from thinking of the way she had behaved in the past years. It was as if she had just realised what she had done. She had always listened to her intuition, something she used to pride herself on. But there was little pride left, now that she realised the extent of her doings. And she knew all too well that God had been extremely kind to her, for no one was hurt yet, apart from Susanne, but Louise did not fault herself for her pain. That was John's doing. He could have ended Louise's and his affair the minute he met Susanne. But of course he had not, and had waited for Susanne to find out. A spineless and selfish man, she thought. Nothing like the caring and honest man August was. But why had she repeatedly betrayed him so easily? How could she have gone behind his back again and again without even a trace of guilt? Surely he must have known or felt something? And if he really did not, does that not prove some sort of lack of interest? Some sort of indifference towards her, his wife? Louise jumped up and paced around the room. She poured herself a glass of his whiskey and turned down the wireless, for her thoughts needed to be heard. Here she was blaming everything on herself, but there is no way August could be guilt-free. She would have noticed immediately if he would have been unfaithful to her. Especially considering the ever-growing carelessness with which she had handled her affair. August had been oblivious throughout all the affairs. He had not noticed the nights away, the secret kisses in the garden at their dinner parties, the letters in their mailbox. What did that say about his love for her? She could have kissed John in front of his nose and he would not have noticed! If he really was that in love with her, Louise thought, he would have not let her out of his sight, and certainly would not have let all the obvious affairs go unnoticed. He did not love her, she decided. He only loved what she stood for. A smart, independent woman who would stand out in the crowd. A prize which he could show off to the world. Not only was he, August, a successful businessman and a worthy townsman, he also had landed himself a first-class wife.

"Well, August," Louise said out loud. "I will not fit into your picture-perfect life anymore. Just you wait."

CHAPTER ELEVEN

After mobilization August did come back safely. Louise had cooled down since the day she had confessed her sins at church. She had continued to go to the Holy Mass and prayed for August to come back safely, but she was nowhere near as happy with her husband as before he had left. She never could let go of the conviction that if he really loved her, he would have known she was not faithful to him. But something had changed in his behaviour that made her soften her opinion about him. He was braver and manlier somehow.

When he came home he had picked her up and kissed her passionately. He had twirled her around and smiled before almost screaming:

"Have you missed me, my darling girl?"

"I have missed you like a pair of lungs for I could not breathe the whole time you were away."

"Oh you do have a knack for drama, Marie Louise."

August laughed, kissed her again and took his wife upstairs. She did not know if it was the impending war or the fact that he had not seen her for so long. But he seemed to be a different man in the bedroom.

"If I did not know better than that there were only men in the army, I would be worried you have been unfaithful to me. It seems that you have gained some moves," Louise said with a giggle.

"Unfaithful to you my love? Never! I have just missed you so very much."

"Well you can miss me more often, dear sir," she cheekily replied. "I like your style."

Louise laughed out loud while August lifted her onto their marital bed that had never been this welcoming before. When he bent over for yet another kiss she grabbed him by the waist and pulled him towards her. She softly bit his lip and looked him in the eyes. There he was, the man she had loved so much throughout the years. Did she still love him? She needed to know. For she thought she had talked herself out of loving him. But seeing his eyes again and feeling his skin on hers made her doubt her revelation. Maybe he did not think badly of her ever, and thus had discarded all suspicions he might have had. Maybe he did care but the thought of Louise betraying just never came to mind, for these were not the kisses of an indifferent man. These were not the touches of a man who did not love. Louise felt her hairs stand up and felt her body shiver like it had not for a very long time. For a moment she lost her train of thought and thought of nothing more than his touch.

That night Louise and August made love like man and wife. And for the first time in their six-year marriage they had both enjoyed it.

~

In the years that followed there was little to laugh about. Roosendaal proved to be an important town in the war as its train station had become a popular target. Roosendaal had been bombed early on in the war and had lost many of its citizens. Men were silently waiting to be called up by the German army as the Netherlands had capitulated from the start. August decided to hide to get out of being conscripted, and took his family to stay with old family friends at a farm a few kilometres from his beloved town. It was here that Louise's love for August ended. She did not know when and she did not know how, but she had felt something shift during that frightful time. She never could pinpoint the exact departure of her love, but she knew she had left it somewhere on that farm. Maybe it was because August fled and hid while others fought in the Resistance, or maybe she just grew tired of him being around all the time. In their marriage they had never been together that intensely for so long. It had been her wish right before the war, but the mobilization pulled them away from each other rather soon after he had made his promise to be home more often. During the war they were together every single day. Every day and every night he was the only adult she saw, and she grew tired over him fretting over her all the time. He had always been protective but knew better than to belittle her. But he had nothing else to do than watch her every move now, and it made her go slowly mad. This man was a downright bore and there was no other explanation. The traits she used to love slowly turned into characteristics she hated. His love for her, his constant need to make her happy, his never-ending inquiries about her health, she longed for her normal life and longed for a new affair. A man who could bring her back into ecstasy. But during the war men were scarce. And the men who were left behind did not dare to defy their wives. War brought out the worst but also the best in people. All of a sudden the most unrefined men turned into Shakespeares overnight.

Louise thought it all to be ridiculous. She had become a bitter woman. Nothing like the upbeat and charming girl she used to be. War had not frightened her, it had bored her. She occasionally seduced August, for she had no other way to fulfil her needs. And the only improvement he had made as a husband was that he had become a better lover. Too little, too late of course, but it was at least something to keep her occupied. She had decided that she would leave August as soon as the war was over. She was not the type of person to stay with someone she did not love. No woman she knew had ever left her husband, but Louise did not care. She never looked at other people when deciding what to do. Louise had planned to leave the Netherlands and leave

August. She would take the children with her and start her life over in a foreign country. Maybe France or even England. It was these thoughts that kept her sane. August's constant nagging left her numb most of the time. She wondered if he nagged as much to his staff. And why he never called her by her name was a mystery to her. Why could he not once use Louise over darling or sweetheart? It was her name after all. No, this man could do no good, no more. She knew she was not being fair, but she could not ignore her body's reaction to him after a while. Sometimes she was nauseated days on end. Just looking at him made her stomach churn. This must be a sign of how bad their marriage had become, Louise thought. It took her weeks before she realized it was not August nauseating her, but his child growing inside her…

Louise cried for two weeks when she realized she was with child again. She did not want this man's baby. She did not want another child at all. She had already given birth to two children and she struggled to feed them in this war. Having money meant a lot less in times of war, and she worried every day whether Betty and Gus would eat enough nutritious food, so they would not be damaged forever. Imagine raising an infant in this world. She had never been able to breastfeed, and she was sure she would not be able to do so this time. Besides, she really wanted to leave August as soon as possible. Giving birth to his child would only slow down the process. She felt sick every time she thought about the child she was growing in her womb. Every cell in her body resented this ill-planned child.

"Oh how happy August will be when I tell him the news," she bitterly thought.

"Another child, but this one is really yours!"

Louise laughed bitterly at her own joke and looked at her growing stomach.

"Oh child, why have you decided to come now into this unhappy family and this awful war? Your life will be not be a fortunate one, I feel. For your first choice has already been one of poor judgment."

CHAPTER TWELVE

Frank was born on the second of November, the gloomy day of All Souls. He was the spitting image of his father. Louise, as a result, suffered from a more severe illness than the one she had had after giving birth to Gus. She did not get out of bed for an entire year. And this time she did not even want to see her new-born baby boy. It seemed she had distanced herself from her entire family. She had ordered a bed in the reception room where she could lie, and had invited an endless stream of family and friends to come and visit her. Anything to set her mind off her family, the war and her marriage. August, Louise and the children had moved back to the townhouse in Roosendaal after they had found out Louise was pregnant again. Roosendaal had not been bombed since the beginning of war, and there were already signs that Germany would yet again lose a world war. Although it was still a frightful time, people gradually got used to their new reality and seemed to have picked up their lives slowly. In Louise's case there was no sign of moving on. By staying in bed she felt she had paused her life, just for a while, so she could resurrect well-rested and well-prepared. But even she did not know what to prepare for. She had never had such a gloomy view on her future before. There she was in a marriage she had tried to revive numerous times, but had failed to do so; and now with a third child who needed her care and attention. She had thought herself to be a strong woman, but for reasons unknown she was not able to handle the situation she was in now. Her plan to leave August had faded as soon as she had found out she was pregnant yet again. There was no way she could leave now with an infant to care for, and no servants to go with her. But her marriage was over, that was the one thing she was sure of. After August and she had gone back home, he had returned to his business again too. This had given her some room to breathe but his absence did not make her heart grow fonder. Quite the opposite, as she resented the evenings more and more.

During the day she often received visitors who spoiled her with flowers. Chocolate or sweets were scarce, but flowers had become an acceptable gift, for people could grow them in their own back gardens. Little Frank was left in the care of Martha, who cherished him like her own. Louise did not care. She did mind, however, that Martha seemed to disapprove of her more and more. It seemed that Martha had apparent issues with Louise's sickbed. And from Martha's point of view Louise agreed her illness did look shady. During the day Louise seemed perfectly capable of concentrating on the newest novels and on entertaining the many guests with her wit and charm. Martha would hear them laugh at Louise's jokes while little Frank

quietly lay in her arms. He seemed more helpless than the other two babies, Martha thought. Maybe because Frank clearly took after his father. Louise's former friend immediately felt attached to the gentle, quiet little Frank. She resented his mother for neglecting this needy infant. Frank was a war child, and it was as if the fears of everyone around him had gotten under his skin. He did not make one noise at night, and seemed only to smile when his father would come home and pull him up to his face to blow him at least a hundred kisses before handing him back over to Martha. Martha and August had shared their concerns for both Frank and Louise. Although August did not see the charismatic Louise that appeared during the day, he did find her illness more worrying, for it seemed insincere. He tried talking to Louise once.
"My lovely, when do you think you will feel better?"
He saw her eyes harden and braced himself for her answer.
"Well I don't know, August. I cannot look into the future just yet, I am still working on that talent."
It was a snide reply, as he had feared.
"Yes I know, darling, but you seem to get by fine during the day. Maybe you could try to get dressed again. See how it will go from there? If you find you cannot go through with it you can get right back to bed."
Louise cringed. If there was something she feared

more than the war, it was the prospective of going back to her marital life. She realized that was the one thing that kept her from leaving her sickbed. Tears ran down her face before she could stop them.

"O darling you don't have to if you are not ready. I am so sorry. You can stay here. But could you maybe feed little Frank yourself again? Martha and I both think he misses his mother."

He should not have mentioned Martha. She knew those two had been talking about her, and she hated them for it. She was a good mother. No one needed to tell her how to raise her children. Gus had turned out fine and she was sick after he was born too.

"So, Martha and you know best? Bring the child then!"

"Louise darling, he is sleeping now. I just meant that we feel he is an infant born in a very insecure world, and the attention of his mother would do him good."

"Well, why don't you make Martha your wife and then she can raise your child. She seems to know everything better."

"Louise. Don't be ridiculous. Stop this nonsense instantly and act like the responsible loving woman I know and love. I will not accept this behaviour. With God as my witness I will get you out of this bed myself if you will not pick yourself up."

Louise swallowed hard. Never in their eleven-year marriage had she seen him this mad. Apparently the man did have a line to cross.

"I have crossed a line, haven't I? I honestly did not know I could ever offend you. I do apologize and I will make an effort to get out of bed."

She did mean what she said, but she did not know how long it would take her to live up to her promise. It was clear, even to her that she had been biding her time but the very thought of everything returning to normal made her stomach churn, and this time she knew for sure it wasn't another baby that made her nauseated. She had not had a lover since John four years ago, and she was slowly turning into a madwoman for it. And there was no way she would make the mistake of sleeping with her husband again.

After that night Louise did feed Frank more often, but she did not bond with him the way she had bonded with Gus and Betty. This child seemed more fragile somehow, but she could not set her mind to really take care of him. She had Gus and Betty to care for as well, and Gus turned out to be a handful. The little nine-year-old had given mischief a whole different meaning. Louise could not count the times he had been sent home from school with extra chores or warnings, and whenever she tried to be strict with him, he made her laugh out loud, so he would not take her punishments seriously. But despite all his tricks and pranks Gus was a very gifted child. No matter how out of control, whenever August or Louise set him behind the piano he would play on it for hours on end. Naturally, they had decided to provide him lessons so he could expand his already-extraordinary talent. Unfortunately the little boy detested the lessons, and pleaded with his mother every single time to not make him go. But she did not give in to her son, and made him go no matter how hard he cried. Gus would usually walk to his teacher's house alone, for it was a short walk of ten minutes. Louise was quite happy when Gus had gone for piano practise, as it provided her with much-needed peace and quiet.

She decided one Wednesday afternoon in May to take Frank to his bed for the first time since he was born. She had slowly started to feel better and was regularly getting dressed again. This was the first day she felt good enough to hold Frank and walk him up the stairs to take him to his room. She held him tight and gazed intensely into his eyes. They were the eyes of August, blue and worrying. His hair was thick and blonde, just like his father's and his upper lip tended to curl upwards, making him look vulnerable. For a moment she warmed up to her baby and leaned in to smell his hair. When she inhaled the strong baby scent her entire house started to tremble. The hard wooden banister started to shake uncontrollably, and she could hear her windows smash. She could not throw herself onto the floor, for she was holding baby Frank. Instead, she cowered down on the stairs and held Frank to her chest. She cried for Martha and Betty, but remembered Betty was out playing at a friend's house. Martha screamed back and said she was in the kitchen. After what seemed like hours, the trembling finally stopped, and Louise dared to crawl back up again. She sat down on the stairs and rocked Frank back and forth in her arms. Then she walked shakily back to the reception room and put Frank in his downstairs crib. She turned on the wireless and heard the worst news a mother could ever hear.

CHAPTER THIRTEEN

"Gus, Gus! Gus is there!" Louise had screamed ever since she heard the news on the radio. The Allied Forces had bombed the milk factory and the house of the piano teacher by mistake. Louise had fallen to her knees and screamed until her lungs protested. After catching her breath she had started to scream again and fought off Martha, who tried to comfort her. August came storming into the house and ran towards her.
"Did Gus go? Did he leave for his lesson? Surely God would not be so cruel."
He fell onto his knees next to his wife and tried to console her when he felt something on his shoulder. He looked up and saw a very concerned Gus standing next to him.
"Why are you both on the floor? Are you that mad that I skipped my lesson? I promise I will go next time, mama. I do."
Louise stared at him with her mouth open. Her screams had turned into soft sobs. For a minute she did not do anything before stumbling towards her son and grabbing him so hard he could hardly breathe.
"You never have to attend one piano lesson ever again."
In fact he could not, for his teacher had died.

~

There was something in the air after Roosendaal was liberated. Even Louise felt it. She thought she would never be able to feel anything else but tiredness for the rest of her life, but there it was: nervous excitement. Butterflies seemed to have occupied her stomach temporarily, and it was hard to find out why. Yes the war was over in this part of the country, but in her pessimistic mind it only meant the beginning of so many other problems. A country that has been on pause for over five years needs an awful lot of work. But for some reason people did not seem to care. Their merriment and enthusiasm even had an effect on Louise, which was rarely ever the case. But as much as she detested it, she too found herself singing softly along to the wireless and dancing along with her ecstatic children. Well, two of them. Frank, who had never seen a world without war, was out of sorts. His mood made more sense to Louise, as she too did not really know what to make of the future that lay ahead of them. And a free world meant a free view on what was to come.

But for some reason she could not let these negative feelings last. It must have had something to do with the air. It sizzled with opportunities. And besides all that, Roosendaal had never been more vibrant. It wasn't much of a secret that she did not really like this

provincial town. But at this point there was not much of a difference between the fairly worldly Breda and this midsized town. Its bars were full and its streets alive with laughter, and there was no better place to be.
So when her old friend Cissy asked her to go to the parade where the Allied Forces would be welcomed, she did not hesitate for long. After years of insecurity, overall numbness and sadness, she felt she deserved to let that part of her have some fun.
When she stepped out of her house right onto the centre of town, she did not even have time to take in the fresh air. Immediately she stumbled upon hundreds of people screaming and waving to passing tanks and trucks full of soldiers. It was daunting for Louise, but she adjusted quickly, having longed for ages for a new adventure. But finding Cissy would be somewhat too much of a challenge. She walked on towards the square and looked for someone she knew. It took her a while before she started to recognise people. It felt like she had been living in a bubble for a year, and it had popped at once leaving her exposed to the world.
"Louise! Turn your head! Come over here!"
The screaming girl could be no one other than Cissy. Cissy had been the only friend apart from Helen who'd really tried to understand Louise's life. She did not of course – Cissy herself loved some gossip and maybe even a party or two, but she would never think of

leaving her safe life behind her or even cheating on her beloved husband. Although at this moment, Louise wasn't so sure. She looked at Cissy's dress, which was way too cold for the cold autumn weather, and her heavily made-up eyes. Her hair wasn't in her usual tight bun, but loosely around her heart-shaped face. Never before had Cissy looked so beautiful and happy. Come to think of it, the girls she was with all looked that happy and gorgeous. Louise wondered if it was the blush powders, or just the mere excitement of meeting young brave shoulders, that had made their cheeks red. Cissy yet again screamed in delight and waved her scarf to the gorgeous young men in the tanks.

Not used to being upstaged by the other women in her town, Louise stepped up her game.

"Come on, let's climb up to one!"

Louise grabbed Cissy by the arm and took her to the middle of the square.

"Excuse me, Sir, would you mind taking us ladies with you through town?"

Louise giggled again and felt her body come to life. She felt Cissy trying to hide behind her, and knew her friend was waiting for her to make the next move. Oh, how sweet it was to be in the lead again; it had been so long! She was so sick and tired of being sick and tired, this was going to be the start of a new era. The new air predicted as much. All of a sudden she felt Cissy being pulled away from behind her. When she turned around she saw her lovely and calm friend being lifted by a bunch of soldiers onto another tank. A pang of jealousy escaped her stomach, but she ignored it. Cissy should enjoy this, she sternly told herself. But the fact was, she could not really get into the same celebrating mood as Cissy so obviously was enjoying. The short high she had felt, quickly evaporated when her friend was pulled away from her. It had brought her great pleasure to help sweet, doting Cissy to a once-in-a-lifetime experience, but for some reason she could not help but feel a little discouraged at this point.

She decided to descend the tank and ignore the shouts of the mainly Canadian soldiers. At first, her plan was to just go home and crawl back into bed, but something stopped her. Although she did feel like a spectator in a museum, from the outside looking into a different era, wondering about the clothing, the ecstatic faces and the drinks that were served, she refused to give up on the idea of feeling the same way as the others. She too had survived the war. She too had been scared to death when little Gus could very well have been dead.

The little monologue in her head had had the wanted effect. Instead of finding her way home, she entered the first bar she saw. It had not been easy to find the actual door to the café because of a pack of soldiers toasting in front of it. Food was still scarce, but alcohol had always been fairly easy to produce, so there was no shortage of strong, home-brewed liquor.

When she finally entered the café, she desperately started looking for any familiar faces. Slowly she began to perspire, which she always did whenever there was any heat somewhere to be found. Her discomfort grew by the minute until she rested her eyes upon a lone soldier near the bar. He seemed to be just as out of place as she felt at this very moment. She tried locking eyes with him, but he turned out to be more interested in the ceiling. He did not look much like a soldier. Although his jaw was strong, his face was way too pale for it to have seen a lot of French or German sun. Also, his posture betrayed a less than athletic build. When he did look up, Louise froze at once. His pale face and frail posture had not prepared her for his piercing brown eyes. They seemed exotic almost and looked at her with such knowledge and confidence. She looked away and tried to search for a hanger to hang up her coat.

"You don't seem to be having a grand old time like the rest of the people. Not that into freedom then are you?"

The soft voice that had whispered these words in her left ear had startled her. Her ear began to glow that very instant, and she tried to hide the redness by

turning her other side to him. How could he have walked towards her this fast? She now started to worry about her perspiration, her flat hair and her lack of make-up, cursing herself for not having had the energy to make any effort this morning.
"I am Jack, by the way."
He oozed so much more confidence than his posture had led her to believe. She still had not uttered a word.
"Would you care for a drink? I am dying to know if you'll be able to form some words after a sip of alcohol."
That triggered her. No one should portray her as a shy nitwit with nothing to say. She was ready for the kill. Wanted to let him know how bright and worldly she was in one sentence. But of course that was much too much pressure for her in these circumstances.
"A drink would be nice, sir, but I am actually looking for my friend."
She hated herself for bringing up Cissy, for she was the last person Louise wanted to find right now, apart from her husband of course.
"Ah, I suppose that's your way of saying I should leave you alone."
Jack bowed his head and backed away slowly, and yet Louise's mind still wasn't working properly. She bellowed:
"No, don't go!"

And without even thinking she grabbed Jack by the arm and pulled him against her, the close contact sending shivers through her body. Her tactics needed some polishing still, but she was not about to give this man up.

"I am sorry, Jack was it? Let us start again."

He did not seem affected by her rough tactics at all. With a dazzling smile he softly pulled away from her and looked her straight in the eye. He swiftly let go of her hand and resumed an appropriate position.

"All right then," he said while getting two glasses with clear spirits in them from a tray that passed by. He took one sip and handed the other glass to her. "Can I get your name? Knowing what to call you might lead to a smoother conversation altogether."

Louise, back at her game, clinked her glass to his.

"Cheers, here's to freedom."

With one eyebrow raised she raised her glass to her mouth and took a big gulp.

"It is Louise, sir. Marie Louise."

"Well, well. Marie L. Lovely to meet you!"

"Marie L?"

"Yes sorry about that. I am still used to using abbreviations I am afraid. What should I call you then? Louise?"

"No, Marie L sounds perfect."

~

Usually Louise would find it the easiest task in the world, entertaining a stranger. It was what she was best at. She prided herself for letting everyone around her feel comfortable. But somehow Jack blocked all her powers. Or so it felt. There was no way to hide, and no way to trick him. It made her vulnerable and confused. For once she did not have any control. Of course she had asked him hundreds of questions. She still knew how to do that, but he had answered staccato and uninterested. He seemed to be solely interested in the way she talked, moved and tried to get herself out of tricky situations. His words were far from flattering, she noticed. He would comment on her creased shirt or the fact that there was lipstick on her teeth. It was obvious he was focusing on only her, but she wasn't sure in what way.

She did not fail to figure out how they were connected though. Some powers no one could block, she thought smugly. Within minutes Louise had found out that Jack was indeed an RAF pilot and was officially an English citizen, but that he in fact was born in Breda like Fons. They even knew each other. Their fathers both had factories in town and often dined together. But Jack was nothing like Fons. Although he had been forward with her, he appeared to be very much on his own. And no matter how hard she tried, there was no way he could be stirred. His boyish humour and mischievous look did not match up to his severe voice and stories at all. But she guessed that was the war speaking. All combatants may have gone through similar experiences, yet every single one reacted on those traumas differently. Jack appeared to be a realistic and rational survivor. He did not deny what had happened but did not dwell on it either. He would rather look forward. But not in the bright optimistic way. He claimed to be more a rationalist than an optimist. More emotional than an optimist, Louise added inaudibly. Without noticing her silent remark, he had gone on about his plans to gain some of the skills he thought he needed in life, but currently lacked.

There was just one way Louise could crack his iron exterior. Whenever she came near him he would clear his throat and fiddle with his hands. He seemed more nervous than the other servicemen did when it came to the womanly attention in the café. To relax him Louise suggested they should go for a walk around the square. She made sure to lead him away from her marital home, so they would not have to touch that subject yet. She had caught him staring at her fingers, and knew all too well that he had seen her wedding band. But there was no time for complicating things now. The parade would leave for another town and Jack would leave with it. And by God was she not letting this opportunity to finally kiss a man again pass by her. All of a sudden he stopped walking and turned to her. Louise automatically leaned forward.

It felt too soon, but nothing had gone according to plan with this mysterious pilot, so she decided to just let him. It did seem a jump from the pleasantries they had been exchanging all night long, but something had shifted during their walk. He seemed to breathe less steadily and seemed to fiddle with his fingers even more. His self-assured voice cracked a couple of times, but he had blamed this on the weather without even blinking. When he turned to her, there was nothing better to do than to close her eyes and brace herself for a passionate kiss from this RAF-man. But the soft sensation on her lips she was expecting did not come. When she was about to open her eyes again, she heard him softly whisper:

"I think you'd better go home Marie L. It is time for me to leave and you should return to your husband."

Jack clumsily shook Louise's hand, and pulled back a strand of hair that had fallen loose in front of her face with the other hand that had hung somewhere near her ears. Louise had trouble opening her eyes. She was stunned. Why in the world did he want to stop? She felt caught as well by his comment about going home to her husband. It made her feel awful. She was sure he thought ill of her. Although the soft stroke of his hand against her face, seemingly by accident but too lovingly for it to not be on purpose, had made her doubt that observation. She just stood there, in front of this introvert soldier and nodded, frantically searching for her voice.

"Well Marie L, I hope to see you again in the future. Maybe old Fons can introduce us properly sometime soon. It would be a downright shame to never see you again."

Jack had gotten back his wits, it seemed. He smiled and let go of her hand he had awkwardly shaken a minute before, then he turned away to re-join his troops. Louise softly said goodbye. After he had left she slowly turned away from the wall she had been standing against the whole time, and walked towards a pack of girls. A phrase she often used when describing a group of women. After all, they usually were as dangerous as a pack of wolves, if not more dangerous.

"Be sure to get your lipstick straight before you go back to your husband, dear," one of the girls sneered.

"Be sure to get your face straight before I go back to your husband, doll." Louise had found her words again.

CHAPTER FOURTEEN

Jack had left his mark on Louise's mood. At once she was up and running again. She had of course little explaining to do as everyone's mood had lifted after the liberation. However, she did underestimate the gossip she had caused. She had expected people to shut their mouths because this time she had not been the only woman in Roosendaal who had not been faithful to her husband; and besides, she thought she had fought off those girls with her comment. Apparently, though, she had only made matters worse, for little Gus had gotten home in quite a state.
"Mama, Hugo says you have kissed another man. He says his mother saw you putting your tongue into a pilot's mouth. How gross."
Louise laughed immediately. She could not help it with little Gus. She was shocked of course, but his face was so stern, and his hands were balled up into fists that he had placed on his hips, which made him look like a little commander. Her giggles also gave her time to think about her answer, for she could not just cast it off. She had been living in Roosendaal for a long time, and she knew that a rumour in this town would only disappear if a bigger and better one came along. She pulled little Gus up onto her lap and stroked his black hair. He had really grown into a handsome young boy, and he would soon be fighting off the girls, although

she was not too sure if there would be a lot of fighting – for she found him to be somewhat of a Casanova already.

"Listen Gus, mama is unlike other mothers you know, and people find that hard sometimes. They tend to make up stories so they can try to understand. So you can be sure that this won't be the last time Hugo will tell you these kinds of stories. But it doesn't matter. You should just shrug and be certain that no matter what, your mother loves you."

Gus shifted from one leg to the other and looked at his mother. He had deep brown eyes, deeper even than Steven's eyes.

"So you did not kiss that pilot man? Or stick your tongue in his mouth?"

For once she would not have to lie to her son. Something that was an incredible relief for once. From a very early age she had always found comfort in his eyes, and he had grown up to be not only her oldest son but also a companion almost. Whenever she had felt down or restless he would calm her by just being Gus. She had hated lying to him from the start, but she felt she had no other choice. It would break his little heart if he knew what his mother had been up to all this time. But this time nothing had happened. A pang of disappointment reached her abdomen. But she swallowed hard and answered her son in the sunniest way she could.

"Well of course not, you silly boy. I would only kiss you!"

And she kissed him all over his face until he screamed and pushed her away.

"I am way too old for that now, mama. If you don't mind please let me go so I can go outside and play."

He was such a comical boy, he almost made her forget the severity of his question. She had never had to deal with keeping her affairs from her children. But Gus was almost ten years old now, and starting to participate in the community on his own account. And although she would probably not see Jack for a long time, she was most certainly planning another encounter. She had already talked to Helen and Fons about him. Of course she had been discreet, but she knew Helen understood immediately. She had asked them if they would invite both her and August as well as Jack to their home in The Hague as soon as the war ended, which would happen any day now surely. Louise had been surprised to find that the rest of the Netherlands was not liberated yet. Roosendaal had been freed for several months now, but the northern parts of the Netherlands had still been occupied during winter, and it had turned out to be the worst winter in history. Fons and Helen had temporarily moved back to Breda, for there was not nearly enough food in The Hague. Even though

Helen and Fons were very well off, they could almost never get their hands on any food in the stores, and with no neighbouring countries nearby, there were no other ways of getting their hands on anything nutritious. They told Louise about people eating flower bulbs and pets, and she screamed in horror. She wanted to do something to help these people but realised there was not much she could do. She knew her request to Helen and Fons was trivial, but they were in desperate need of some light entertainment anyway while they feared for their friends and families' lives up north. Louise would often visit to keep their minds distracted, or would listen to the horrible stories they told her. She hated the war but loved that it had brought her back her friends, for she was in desperate need of friendly faces. Her marital home had grown colder over the years, and the town had been gossiping non-stop about her escapades. Little Frank had proved to be a true war child and suffered from a lot of illnesses, and to anyone's surprise Betty had grown out of her silent ways and turned out to be quite a chatterbox. Gus as always was a handful, and played the piano for hours on end, driving August mad. A big music lover himself, he could just not understand that his oldest son showed zero interest for his beloved classical music. To top it all off, Martha had never forgiven Louise for neglecting Frank during the first year of his life, so there was no one left to laugh, cry or even talk with. Louise felt incredibly lonely sometimes.

But meeting Jack had done wonders. Mysterious, introverted, passionate Jack. She would regularly lose her train of thought and fall into a deep daydream that would make her whole body shiver. It had done her so much good, for she felt like her old self again. She could even find the strength to treat August as her husband again. A fact that he very much appreciated. Of course he did not have a clue as to why his wife was in good spirits again, but he figured it had something to do with the liberation. It was why he was merrier anyway. The future seemed bright again and his biggest fear, losing his family, was gone. After what had happened to Gus' piano teacher, August had not been able to sleep for weeks. He would wake up screaming in the middle of the night covered in sweat, and immediately check if every one of his children was all right. But luckily all was well now, and he was able to look to the future again.

CHAPTER FIFTEEN

The harsh feelings she had developed towards August during the war softened somewhat. Ever since she was able to come out of bed again and get into her own routine, his presence did not seem to annoy her as much. It helped that August was working long hours again, and that whenever they saw each other, she saw him as a father. And no matter how vile she thought him, he was the best father she had ever seen up close. That included her own father, whom she loved to pieces and who was known for his warm and liberal approach to raising his children. But August was the most caring man when it came to his children. It came as no surprise that Frank turned out to be his favourite. Not only for the obvious reason, the fact that this was the first child to share his genes, but also because he felt that this unlucky child had suffered a lot since the day he was conceived. His mother had not been on a nutritious diet when she was carrying him, and therefore little Frank was born with little fat on his baby bones. He came out tall and scrawny and was not able to grow into a healthy baby, seeing as his mother had been unable to breastfeed him and regular milk was extremely scarce during the war. To make matters even worse, his mother had felt ill for nearly a year starting the day after he was born, and had not been able to care for him like she had been for the other two.

August took it upon himself to provide the little boy the love his mother was no longer inclined to give him. It had formed a bond that turned out to be unbreakable. Unreachable even, according to Louise. She felt as though Frank and she had gotten off on the wrong foot from the start, and looking at the pair of them made her wonder if she could ever re-join the race. But for some reason she did not mind as much as she should have. It must have been God's plan to keep her distance from this baby, she later on concluded.

But the love August showed to Frank had taken her back to days when she still loved August. Somehow there was still some of it left, she had just needed to meet someone else to rekindle it. How ironic, she muttered to herself. It seemed as though there had been no other way to feel somewhat content in her marriage than to find a third party to share it with. The biggest marital crisis had been in fact when she had been without a lover for over 3 years. The moment she had met Jack, she immediately had warmed up to her husband again. A cruel mechanism, she decided.

But it was the excuse she needed to pursue another rendezvous with this mysterious pilot. She did not know how or when, but she did know she would definitely see him again. Of course she had asked Helen to arrange a meet-up, but Helen did not know where to start. She did not know him personally, and did not want to drag Fons into this web Louise had spun yet again for herself. She did, however, find out that Jack would visit Roosendaal on a regular basis. His uncle and aunt lived there, and after the war he found comfort in visiting them as often as he could. Helen did not know anything about this bond, but she did know where they lived.

Louise, not a stranger to obsessions, formed a plan close to madness so that she could run into him again. She registered herself as a volunteer nurse in the hospital next to where his uncle and aunt lived. She offered to take care of the wounded soldiers who still remained there, and promised to cook them some meals too. She went there mainly during the weekends, seeing as though it was the most logical time for Jack to visit. And finally, after weeks of actually enjoying the volunteer nursing she ran into him. True to form she had not thought of a plan for what she would do or say if the moment ever occurred. So when she did see him pull up his car to the new townhouse across the street, her first thought was to make a run for it. She had once read about the 'fight or flight' impulse animals had. Hers would definitely be run, for whenever things got tough, an ominous feeling would arise in her gut, and move its way up to her head until there was nothing left to do than move her feet as fast as she could. So when she saw Jack's dark blond hair emerge from his car, she did not wait for his head to follow it, but turned her head and started to walk briskly to her bicycle. He called after her and ignored her attempts to avoid him. It was moments like these that made her sure that the feelings were mutual.

~

"Don't you reckon?" Louise suddenly realised she was supposed to answer, but had no idea of what Jack had asked her. Ever since he had suggested to go and sit on a bench nearby and talk for a while, Louise had been fantasising about his lips instead of paying attention to the words they had formed. She had not focused on what he was saying exactly, but mainly on the way he was saying it. How he moved his tongue against his teeth when he spoke, for example. She had noticed that whenever he was interested in something, he would get carried away and frantically move his lips to catch up to the words that would come tumbling out of his mouth. To avoid stuttering, he placed his tongue firmly against his lower teeth. It fascinated her, for he was not usually a man of many words. At least, she had not witnessed him being this talkative yet. He did not wet his lips during the monologue, Louise noticed. That was fortunate, she thought, for she detested men who had wet lips. They reminded her of her first kiss. It was with the sweetest boy ever but whenever he talked, two white little puddles of saliva would form around the outer edges of his mouth. He would therefore use his tongue every odd minute to remove the excess saliva. Whenever he kissed her she would brace herself for the amount of moisture that came her way, and the thickness of his tongue. It had put her off from kissing for over two years.

She was lost in her thoughts when Jack asked for her opinion about something. Luckily she was a fast thinker. She remembered he had started a story about his father's hat factory, and that he would love to build one just like it abroad. She went with her gut feeling and trusted the sparkle in his dark brown eyes. "It would be a grand idea!" He looked at her and shook his head. His eyes lit up even more and the wrinkles around them became visible. "You weren't paying attention, were you? How is it that a woman as bright as you can get distracted so easily?" He was dead serious. And of course she could not explain herself to him. What should she have said? That she had fallen madly in love with him from the moment she had laid eyes on him? That she was unable to concentrate on anything other than his physical appearance and the timbre of his voice? That she was willing to leave her husband and three children for him? Instead she acted outraged: "I was paying attention to you, honestly! But you talk so fast! If you must know, I can hardly make out the words you're saying. You are a true mutterer." He looked at her and she felt naked. He somehow knew she was lying. How odd, she thought. She was the best liar known to man. From a young age Louise had learned that people will always believe compliments and insults, no matter how unlikely they may seem. She on the other hand never believed any form of flattering or criticism, except when she knew it to be true herself. She had not known Jack long, or well for that matter. But she did suspect he was not as self-assured as he might seem. So what had made him see through her lie? It captivated her, the way he treated her. For somehow she knew from the very moment they had locked eyes that he looked at her differently. She had felt scared and safe all at once. It seemed as though he was one of the very few people not captured by her strong appearance, but instead touched by her softer, clumsy and tender side. A side she carefully hid from everyone. Everyone except sometimes August.

August too had fallen for that soft, smart but clumsy girl. And now, after years of marriage he would still almost be pleased when she would fall ill or when something bad happened to her. For she would forget about her 'woman of the world'- exterior and be his little girl for a while again. But August did truly love both sides of her. She had often asked him if he would be happier with a woman who would just take care of him, who would get his slippers when he would get off work. A woman who would cook his meals every single day and not only on special occasions, someone who would take care of him. Unlike Louise, who was kind but definitely not a very nurturing and caring wife. But he would always tell her that he would turn into this boring and well-balanced man if he had married such a girl, and he would later on hate himself for it. There was no one who was prouder of her than August was. But besides him there was no one open to her softer, more vulnerable side. She did not mind, she was far from fond of those traits. She hated her clumsiness. And the last thing she wanted to become was an obeying and caring wife. But she did feel tired of always being in charge. Of always having to carry all the responsibilities. She was the eldest in her family and behaved like one as well. She ran her own home and the homes of her parents, brother and little sister. And everyone knew she did not care for any help at all. But sometimes, every once in a blue moon, she just longed for someone who would take away her worries, stroke her hair and promise her that everything would be all right. Jack gave her that feeling. And although from the outside she gainsaid every single statement he made about her, from within she knew he had revealed her well-hidden wishes during the few moments he had spoken to her. That scared and excited her more than she could handle. She had fallen in love before, madly even, but she had never experienced so much turmoil because of it before. Maybe it was the situation, maybe it was his piercing brown eyes, maybe she felt vulnerable because the war had just ended. But for the first time in ages she did not know what to do with her

feelings. She did not know anything.
He saw her startled expression and started to chuckle. "You are something, you know that? I don't think I have ever met anyone like you." Louise smiled like she had not smiled in ages and softly answered: "Likewise." Her voice was raw and vulnerable. She stared at her shoes and shyly looked up to him. "Well that is something I will not believe, Marie L! I am just a run-of-the-mill kind of fellow. You know, the simple kind that has happened to have survived the war in an aeroplane. You on the other hand are a remarkable woman. I could tell this from the moment I met you." His tone was friendly, but distant. Louise panicked a bit. He sounded so matter-of-factly while she was searching for words and her voice. The last time she remembered being this shy for words was when she was still a child. Of course, she was not always as loud as people knew her to be, but shy? It was a feeling that felt foreign to her. And yet he was showing no sign of insecurity or vulnerability. What if she was feeling all these feelings in vain? What if she would be willing to throw her life away for someone who was polite and friendly to her, but did not love her back? Her stomach dropped and suddenly she felt nauseated. "I am truly sorry, Jack. But I really need to be heading home soon. We have dinner plans. My husband and I do." He looked at her, and for the first time since their

conversation began he did not smile. He looked disappointed even. Louise wasn't sure if he was disappointed in the fact that she needed to go back to her husband, or that he could not finish his story, the story she had not even listened to. She went for the latter explanation and in a friendly way stroked his thigh. "The next time we see each other you must tell me all about your plans to build a factory abroad. It sounds thrilling!" His face opened up again. "That would be wonderful, Marie L." He abruptly stood up from the bench they had been sitting on, leaving her hand to hover a few inches above the spot on the green wood where his thigh had been. Louise looked at her hand. It was starting to tremble slightly, and she quickly pulled it back into the pocket of her winter coat. "I should have worn gloves," she half-heartedly said to explain her trembling fingers. "Yes girly, you really should have. You will get a cold if you don't take proper care of yourself. Let this be a lesson." His voice sounded stern but his face was still portraying his friendly, open and handsome features. He was taller than he appeared to be, she noticed. Especially when he stood straight, like now. Up to this day she had not seen him standing straight. Not willing to let him leave with the winning hand, she looked at him fiercely and told him: "Glad to see you standing up straight. You know? You shouldn't crouch your back like you normally do. You'll be sorry when you're older when you keep walking like that." He shook his shoulders and formed his body into the position she had come to know and love. His head bent slightly forward and his upper back in an almost horizontal position. He awkwardly waved to her, right in front of her face, and startled her with this sudden movement. He then turned away from her. He did not look back once. Louise felt like she could not move. She stood right next to the bench and watched him getting smaller and smaller as he walked away. She did not know when she would see him again.

CHAPTER SIXTEEN

Louise had become accustomed to lying to her husband. In an early stage of her marriage she had split her life with August from the life she led with other men. She did not had the intention of ever leaving August anymore. She could not imagine a life without him. Of course, their marriage was far from perfect, but she could not imagine loving anyone the way she loved August, and vice versa. For he was truly a doting husband without idolising her too much. He acknowledged her flaws and knew how to disarm her unreasonable episodes in one smooth swoop. Louise was a temperamental woman before she met August, but ever since they became a couple she had learned to dial down the urge to put up fights all the time. She did not so much as suppress those feelings, they just subsided when in August's presence. She had suffered from long periods of illnesses that involved not getting out of bed for feeling blue most of the time. And during those months she had worked out that being near August was the best medicine. Of course, she blamed August for a lot of her pain. But that was mainly because she found it easier to look for the root of her problems in someone else, than to admit that her own character and lack of it was the real reason for her feelings. In fact there was no one else in the world who could soothe her pain. Even when it came to heartaches that were due to other men. So when Louise finally got the strength to turn her eyes away from the direction Jack had walked in, she decided that she would indeed head home to have an intimate dinner with her husband. Ever since the war had ended, they both had been so busy with meeting up with friends and trying to get better food from the borders who were now free of the Germans, that they had not had the chance to really sit down together for a meal. Little Gus and Betty were 11 and 7 years old, and they did everything in their powers to get the attention of their parents. Frank was still a toddler and a rarely quiet one as well. He seemed to be the most happy and chatty whenever his father was near him. He was easily ignored and therefore Louise saw it through that little Frank would get some alone time with his father every single day. All this made it hard for August and her to have time to themselves. But this night Louise needed him. She needed him to stroke her hair or to just be near her. Just his calm breathing would be enough. She opened the door and took in the last breath of fresh air. August was a heavy smoker, and the house was usually packed with a thick cloud of smoke when he was home. She arrived past office hours, so the house was already full of the blue circles of his Amateur cigarettes. The house felt packed with energy. Something she was not up to this evening. She heard

some giggles coming from the kitchen, and had a hard time finding room for her coat on the hanger, because of a thick coat that seemed to take up the entire space. For a moment she considered taking off her shoes and quietly going up the stairs to avoid the company that obviously had filled her home with laughter. But she knew better than to climb into bed, for that would mean she would have to explain herself to August. And of course she could fake a headache or other womanly illness, but the end-of-war celebrations had put everyone including Louise in such an ecstatic mood that it would not be really believable. Besides, she did not think she could manage to fabricate another lie. So she took one look in the mirror in her hallway, pinched her cheeks and ruffled her hair with her still-freezing fingers. She straightened her back and took a deep breath.
"What on earth is all this noise I am hearing?" Louise jokingly said when she entered the living room.
"Mother!" Gus almost tumbled over when he ran over to give her a big hug. Betty graciously followed her older brother and shook her little head.
"Boys," she sighed, and Louise couldn't repress a giggle. Betty looked at her blankly and gave her a quick peck on the cheek. "Frank has been playing with his train all day long. Again. I don't know how boys can get preoccupied with the same toy for days in a row," Betty

stated in a posh voice.

"By God child, where have you learned to talk like that? And besides, when you were two years old you weren't up to much more than playing with your doll either. So don't flatter yourself, girly."

The mention of the word 'girly' brought her back to a few moments ago, when Jack had pointed out that she should have worn gloves. She remembered his stern and distant tone paired with his soft expression and beaming smile. Her stomach felt weak and a warm stream of butterflies filled her abdomen. She daydreamed further about his lips, his voice and his smell when August entered the room. He had been in the wine cellar and looked rather pleased with his pick.

"Darling wife, where were you? We have rather important company this evening, have you noticed?"

Louise trembled and looked at the goose bumps that had formed on her arms. She got up from the floor after cuddling both Gus and Betty again, and she smiled.

"August! You look pleased. Picked out a fine wine again? And do tell me about this special guest. I cannot wait to see who you want to serve this special wine to." She often lovingly ridiculed his love for wine. She did not really care for all the specifics. A wine was either good or bad, and to be told the specifics of every single Beaujolais before she so much could have a sip of it, bored her sometimes. But she loved his enthusiasm, so decided to go along with his happy mood tonight. She kissed his greasy forehead lovingly and let him escort her to the sitting room, where a vaguely familiar man was sitting. Without his rope she did not recognise him immediately, but when he stood up to say hello to her she suddenly knew: The Bishop was here.

"What an incredible surprise," she cried out a bit too loudly. His visit had taken her by surprise. The last thing she needed tonight was a dinner filled with religious chatter. She already had a hard time justifying her infidelities without being reminded of the religious views on cheating on one's spouse. And Louise was still, despite everything, a very Catholic woman. To her it had never been a problem to combine both worlds, but anyone else would have a hard time understanding why a deeply religious woman could be so promiscuous and reckless. She had always felt that she understood the Lord better than most, and that as long as she had a pure heart, He would understand. She deeply respected Bishops and other servants of God, and therefore tried to translate her feelings into a way they would understand as well. That usually went well, for they were not immune to her charms. But she was not sure if she could hold up another masquerade in this state. But of course she did. She never ceased to amaze herself when it came to putting up false fronts. For some reason she was always able to pull herself together in front of anyone who was not as close to her as her family or husband was. Usually it took her a minute or so to get into character, but after a while she even convinced herself she was more than fine. It was like every bad feeling just subsided to the background, and eventually even left her body until something happened that freshened her memory.

"Shall we retire to the sitting room, your Excellency?" August asked eagerly. Louise knew August was keen to open up the bottle of wine he had carefully picked out, and to see the reaction of the Bishop. The Bishop had been declining wine all evening, and Louise was a bit worried that August would be let down by the Bishop's reaction. But at least she had the dining room to herself for a minute. She poured the last of the white wine into her glass and took a large sip. She had already drunk two glasses during dinner, something she usually did not care for during the week. The children were still awake, and she wanted to stay sharp in front of them. They already had a father who usually slurred his words after 6 pm; it would not be a desirable development for their mother to show similar behaviour. But this evening the wine seemed to offer the support she so desperately needed. And since she would not get any from her husband, alcohol seemed a good alternative.

She heard her husband pull the cork and proudly expound on the age and the taste of wood of this deep red Beaujolais. The fluid that hastily left the bottle made that rich sound wine makes when it's poured into a thin wide glass. She heard the bishop mutter something and sat up straight when she heard footsteps coming towards her. The door opened and August stormed in. He looked flustered. His eyes were wide open, and when he noticed her sitting at the table he whispered inaudibly.
"What is it that you are saying, dear?" Louise whispered back.
"He, he wants water with his wine to soften the taste!" August yelled in a whisper. Louise saw the pain in his eyes and immediately felt sorry for August. He really was a child sometimes. She had never met anyone who did not alter his or her tactics towards people once they grew older. Except for August. He still was as open to everyone as five-year-olds usually are. He had zero prejudices, no reservations with anyone or any situation whatsoever. A naïve trait of him she truly loved. But the disappointment that came with it was horrendous to witness. It was like explaining to Gus why someone would be so mean as to steal his favourite toy car. She stood up from the table, which made her realise that the last glass of wine was really one too many. She placed both hands on the rim of the antique table she'd

inherited from her great aunt, and she walked clumsily towards her husband. She still had not taken off her heels and although she wore heels every single day, she was known to trip with them on a regular basis. She finally reached the highly disappointed August and kissed his forehead yet again. She smiled at him:

"You know that bishops tend to mix their wine with water? Probably hoping it will turn into more wine so they can call themselves a regular Jesus Christ." Louise chuckled quietly and although she knew she was risking taking this joke a bit too far, she saw in his eyes that August appreciated this slightly inappropriate joke. She walked towards the kitchen and grabbed a tumbler and filled it with water.

"Here you go. Just make sure you enjoy your glass. And if he wants some more, come back here and pour him some of last night's red wine instead. I'll join you in a minute and I'll make sure to savour every single sip of that divine Beaujolais. I promise."

His lips formed a soft smile. Louise noticed that August's eyes did not light up the way Jack's did when smiling. Immediately her thoughts went back to this afternoon. She imagined her hand back on his thigh, but this time Jack would not get up. He would stare back at her, softly take her hand in his hand and braid his fingers through hers. He would hold his hand up, taking hers with him and release it just so he could use

his hand to stroke her face. He would laugh, softly bite his lip and move his face close to hers. She would use her thumb to gently pull his lip from under his teeth, and slowly stroke his lower lip, his chin and then playfully use her index finger to trace the buttons of his coat. He would then moan softly and suddenly pull her towards him. Slowly he would bring his nose up to hers.
"I'll take the tumbler, dear," August said when he gently pulled the glass bottle from her hands. "You get your rest and join us whenever you are ready to. I love you, darling. You always know how to cheer me up."
August turned away and opened the door in a more cheerful way than a minute before. Louise sat back down and softly banged her head onto the table.
"What are you doing, mother? It looks ridiculous." Betty stared at her in this wise ladylike manner as if she was the older person, forever teaching the proper ways of how to behave.
Louise looked up and smiled at her only daughter. "I was banging my head because someone is still up at bedtime!" She ran over to Betty, steadier than the first time she had gotten up from the table, and grabbed the little girl. Betty screamed when Louise lifted her, and the girl giggled all the way up to her room. When Louise put her to bed she kissed the wise little girl with the raven black hair and whispered:

"My beautiful little baby, don't become like me. Promise me that."

But Betty had her eyes closed already, and her breathing was getting heavier. When Louise walked backwards towards the door she heard Betty murmur: "But you are the best mother. You truly are."

If only you knew, Louise thought. If only you knew. She closed the door and used up every last little bit of willpower to not return to her bedroom, but to go downstairs to accompany August and the bishop.

CHAPTER SEVENTEEN

Seducing Jack became Louise's number one goal. It became a true obsession. It surprised her that even in her thirties she was still able to become so addicted to love. It had always been her weak spot. In general Louise was quite relaxed. Well-balanced even. But when it came to love she appeared to have no rational bone in her body. When she was an adolescent she had quite liked the passion that being in love triggered in her. But when she grew older it became more and more of an Achilles heel. When she was young and carefree her obsessive side could not do much harm. Her manipulative ways still seemed naïve in a way. People tended to believe she would grow out of her dramatic episodes. But she did not. She did get better at hiding her feelings though. But that did not make them less dominant. Instead they made her feel alone. She could not share with anyone how she felt. No one would understand why she could not ignore what her body was telling her. That she was a primitive creature when it came to love, unable to withstand the desires of the flesh. They thought it childish to let one's feelings lead one's life. Once a person has chosen a path he must stick to it, seemed to be the overall mantra. But she did not have a clue as to how to ignore what was going on inside her. She envied the women who could easily set aside their own wishes in order to keep their family happy. Well, in a way she did. She pitied them as well. For she was not among those who believed in sticking to a chosen path. She simply could not imagine that ignoring such strong urges would be considered healthy or even normal. It was like ignoring an air raid siren during war times. As soon as you hear that noise that drowns out all thoughts known to men, there's one option left: duck or run. And that's the only two options Louise seemed to have when it came to love, hide it or run away. For the past decade she had unconsciously chosen to hide her feelings and lead a double life. She did not think she was able to do that a third time. This time she felt her first response to the air raid siren would be to run.

However, it had surprised Louise how easy it had been to split her two lives without feeling too guilty. As long as you push your limits gradually, there'll hardly be any remorse at all, Louise had found out. She was not proud of this revelation. Instead it was the reason she still felt guilty from time to time. Or a bad person even. She had been raised with the idea that humans are warm and forgivable creatures. That a person would always try to do the right thing. An odd message her parents had given her, Louise thought. Especially given the fact she had been alive during two horrible wars. But her parents still seemed to think in terms of good or bad, and so did everyone else. It had made her feel different and evil sometimes when she was spending her time with Steven or John.

But lately she had a more laissez-faire approach to the subject. She still believed in good and bad, but she also believed that people determined their own boundaries in a way that seemed convenient. So she had decided to determine hers in a convenient matter too. And ever since this decision had been made, Louise felt more at ease with her own yearnings. Unfortunately, the yearnings towards Jack brought up a whole different kind of problem. For Jack seemed to have no interest in answering Louise's longings. There were moments she was convinced he did, but she was not entirely sure. He was a kind and polite man, and any chivalry could be an outcome of one of those traits. But then there was the smothering look in his eyes sometimes, and the way he bit his lip when he looked at her. And more important: the way he spoke of her flaws, her clumsiness, and her impatience. For some reason he seemed to find the way she lived her life fascinating. He could describe the exact details on how Louise would have said one thing very passionately at one point, and how she would gainsay every statement she had made an hour later. He would point out playfully the discrepancies of what she had said, and he would shake his head. He would open up that handsome face of his and lovingly add: "you weird little woman of mine."

Whenever he called her 'his', the floor would disappear from underneath her feet and her blood would drop to her knees immediately, leaving her nauseated and pale. But as soon as she would try to confess to him that she had feelings for him, he would somehow find a way to change the subject or worse, leave in a slight hurry. So Louise kept on plotting little schemes in her head to arrange another meeting with Jack. Something that needed a lot of creativity on Louise's part.

Although Jack had stopped flying for the RAF, he did go back and forth to England a lot. The reason was a reason Louise wished to ignore. Of course she knew he was married, to a woman in the army in fact. And it should not have bothered her. She herself was married. Steven was. It had never been an issue before. But this time the very thought of Jack being married made her sick to her stomach. It even made her think vicious thoughts of the woman, whom she had never met. She once had promised herself to never talk ill of another woman. She had often been the subject of a rumour mill and she had sworn not to return the favour. She honestly did not understand why women had the insufferable urge to talk bad about each other. According to her it was the reason women were the weaker sex. But for some reason she had formed an opinion of Jack's wife without even meeting her once. Maybe it was because Jack did not show enough interest in Louise. And she could not figure out why, for he seemed to be at ease with her whenever they were together. More so than when he was with other people, Louise had noticed. He once even told her that he felt he could be his true self around her, but for some reason it did not urge him to try and see her more often. She would always be the one who initiated their rare meetings. And the only reason she could come up with for this lack of initiative from his side was the fact that he was married. The fact that he did not feel more than a dear friendship for her was simply ridiculous. She had never felt such a strong chemical reaction as when she was near him. The mere smell of him sent her to ecstasy in a matter of seconds; surely he must have felt the same?

But like August, Jack was a good man. A strict Catholic who was less prone to seductions than she was. Why was she always attracted to men who could restrain themselves? Was it because she was jealous? Or did she just find the challenge she needed with these right-path kinds of fellows? A combination of both, she suspected. Nothing made her long for a man more than the fact the he was unavailable and unreachable. She found this strange, for she had no such urge to win when it came to anything else. As soon as situations became difficult, Louise usually backed out. She wasn't a typical winner although she did love to play games.

School had always been easy for her. Luckily, because she would not have put any more effort into it than she had. But when it came to men there was no better contestant for the first prize than Louise. She would never give up, she would go on until every single referee, contester and in fact the prize itself had given up. Unfortunately, whenever in said situation Louise did not know how to stop. And she knew that she was capable of destroying every single good thing in her life.

So although nothing had happened yet, she was scared of what the future would hold. But not scared enough to stop pursuing Jack. She simply couldn't. Jack was the first thing she thought of when she woke up, and the last face she saw when she closed her eyes at night. Even Gus' lovable brown eyes made her think of Jack's piercing pair. In fact, Louise found it hard to think of anything other than Jack's bent shoulders, his wavy thick dark blond hair and his pale skin. Every time she went into town to go for a drink or to do some shopping, she thought she saw him walking across the street or talking to someone she knew. All of a sudden Louise developed a light hatred of men's hair fashion. There seemed to be very little variety when it came to the art of cutting the hair of a man. Every single fellow in Roosendaal had the same side part and length, or so it seemed. It drove Louise crazy sometimes. She knew it would be unlikely to run into Jack in her hometown. But her fantasies sometimes were so incredibly real to her, that it was hard to know when her fantasy stopped and reality began. She knew the only way to temporarily stop the madness was to meet up with him again. But how? He had stopped visiting his aunt and uncle on a regular basis because he was spending all his free time at the hat factory of his father. Helen had not been in touch with him either, and she did not know anyone else who could have been of any help. So until she had some sort of plan, her fantasies were all she could live off. She did not have the peace of mind to really sit down and write for longer than 10 minutes, but if she had, she would have the potential of becoming a great novelist. She imagined if she had been able to write down the endless conversations, heated rendezvous and detailed descriptions of Jack's body, she would have a downright bestseller on her hands. But she could not even sit down to read at this stage. If she would not be eating every cake or biscuit she had gotten her hands on lately, she would definitely have lost a couple of pounds, for she was forever on her feet. All of a sudden she cleaned up after dinner, took up gardening and started doing some of the daily chores Martha usually did. She simply could not sit still or talk to anyone else besides Cissy. She was afraid she would start talking about Jack, and then she would not know

how to stop. So instead she stayed busy and far away from social events. A challenge for this holiday season because people were beside themselves. They did not have lots of means to throw an actual party, but the fact that they were able to freely meet up after hours had been enough reason to keep on partying for days on end. A development Louise usually would encourage and sponsor. But this time she could not bear to meet up with all these gleeful, hypocritical faces. Suddenly it seemed publicly accepted to enjoy life, to behave a bit silly, to not strut in line all the time. We are free now, so we should be able to do whatever, seemed to be the general mantra. Total nonsense, Louise thought. She had been living her life by that motto ever since she could talk, but people had never accepted her lifestyle. She was glad that these uptight people finally had found their happiness, but she sure as hell would not celebrate this revelation with them.
That all changed when she received an invite in the mail from Breda.

CHAPTER EIGHTEEN

She discovered the invite a few days after it arrived with the post. Well in fact, it hadn't been Louise who had made the discovery, but Helen. Louise had made it a habit to only search for personal letters in the mail. The never-ending stream of invites, business propositions and bills that the postman delivered to her doorstep two times a day had made her a sloppy reader. She usually scanned the pile of envelopes for a letter from Helen or, in vain, from Jack, and saved the rest for Martha or August to read. Although Helen had temporarily moved back to Breda, Louise and she had kept up their tradition of letter-writing. It was like writing a diary, Louise thought. A safer version, for these words would leave the house and therefore could not be found by her husband. Or Gus. Especially since she had met Jack, those letters had become an outlet of her feelings. She could sit down just long enough to pen down her latest emotions. Putting them on paper had a sort of liberating effect on Louise. Reading back what she had written to Helen made her see things more clearly. The words would sometimes order her feelings about Jack, and the feelings Jack may or may not have for her. It pained her to write down Jack's rejections, but then again she could always soften the blow by describing his nonverbal messages. At the end of the letter the outcome was always the same: Jack must love her back but was afraid to admit his true feelings for her. How could he not? Sure, he had never kissed her or told her he loved her, but did he really have to? Wasn't it enough that he stared at her when he thought no one was watching? Or that he would always touch her hand whenever she handed him something? Of course he would not tell her he had feelings for her. He was a straight man, a faithful man unlikely to betray his wife. But she was sure that when he would just spend more time with her, he would see that there was no escaping the chemistry they had. She needed to be very clear about her wishes towards him. Only then would he be inclined to open up himself to her. There was no other explanation than that he was scared. Scared of her rejection, scared of devastating his wife, his family. And she had more at stake, he knew. She had three children, one of them still a toddler. He was only being a gentleman by not divulging his love. He had left the choice up to her. And therefore she must be in the lead. Of course she sometimes thought these theories to be a bit farfetched, but they felt logical on paper. And besides, Helen shared her point of view.

Usually it did not take Helen long to respond. Helen loved Louise's stories about the men she met. Helen on the other hand was as loyal to Fons as a dog was to its owner. But that did not mean that Helen frowned upon Louise's actions. She and Cissy were always pretty liberal about it. In fact they seemed to enjoy it more than a women's magazine. That suited Louise, but she made sure that the letters weren't all about her. She genuinely missed her friend who was married to her ex-fiancé. And she was very interested in how they were doing. They were lucky enough to have escaped from The Hague right before the Hunger winter had started. But a lot of their friends were still there, and so Helen's worries were far from over. In Helen's last letter she had told Louise that the letters she had written to her friends had been sent back in one package after a few days. She wasn't sure if it was because of the weather, the war, or because they weren't living in their houses anymore. Even though the South of the Netherlands was freed, the misery of war was far from over.

Louise was eating her breakfast when she received Helen's latest letter. As always, she ate breakfast in the dining room after the children were off to school. She was still in her morning gown, being everything but a morning person and Martha, like every morning, toasted some bread and spread the slices with butter and jam – something she had picked up during one of her travels to England. She had even bought the toaster there, a novelty in good old Roosendaal. After Martha made her coffee, she often fetched the mail and handed it to Louise. An exchange which involved no talking from either side. Louise often listened to the wireless while perusing the mail, and Martha carried on with cleaning up the kitchen.

"A letter from Helen, ma'am," Martha stressed the name Helen and raised her eyebrow slightly.

O that nosey woman, Louise thought. She knew Martha could well drink Louise's blood and would happily be August's wife if the situation would occur. Louise suspected that was why Martha watched Louise's every move and looked for clues of unfaithfulness in every nook and cranny in the house. Louise was sure that Martha thought it possible for Helen's letter to be from someone else than Helen indeed, and she strived to keep that insane theory alive.

"O, Helen!" Louise overreacted. "I cannot wait to read what she has to tell me. Let's open up this beautiful envelope and find out!" She opened the letter in a secretive way on purpose, and began to blurt out some obvious frivolities in the letter.

"Ah she tells me her mother's doing well!" Martha had already gone back to her kitchen, but Louise found it too amusing to stop.

"She said she tried to make my famous pudding for a dinner party but failed miserably, that daft girl. I already told her that she needs to practice before serving such a complicated dessert at a party."

Her last words were slurred and broken off quickly. In fact Helen was not writing about the pudding, but about an invite she had found in the mail. An invite from Jack's father.

"Martha, Martha!" Louise yelled a little too loudly. "What have you done with the invites we have received this week?"

It took Martha ages to get back from the kitchen. She was as slow as she was fat, Louise thought bitterly.

"What invites, ma'am?" she ignorantly responded. "Have you got a specific one in mind?"

"Oh I bet you would want to know what invite I am talking about, you annoying ship of a woman," Louise muttered out of earshot.

"None in particular, just the ones from this week. Helen wants me to drag her to one of these parties."

Louise almost patted herself with glee for this wonderful made-up excuse. She truly was at her best when in love. Sharp and fast on her feet.

"Well, I suggest you 'drag' Helen to a party to which you might receive invites today. I have RSVP'd all of the ones from this week and thrown them away."

Louise was sure she saw a smile form around Martha's mouth. And she knew she had to be careful now. Coming across too eager would seal the deal in Martha's eyes, and she did not believe that she could lie to August again. She was done lying to this man who had done nothing but love her for the last decade.

"Well that slims down our options, but I am sure we

can manage, Martha. Job well done by RSVP'ing. We don't want to be rude of course. And those invitations do make a fine base for the fire don't they," Louise jokingly added.

"They certainly do, ma'am," Martha sighed and retired back to the kitchen.

Well at least she knew where Martha had thrown away Jack's invitation. How could she have been so stupid as to overlook this invite? It was after all from Breda. That must have stood out? Well apparently not, Louise bitterly thought, and drank her last sip of coffee. Cold, as always. She clenched her teeth while she felt the cold liquid pass her throat, and she let out a little dramatic "ah." Then she stood up from the table that was already cleared except for her plate and cup. Usually she carried the plate back to the kitchen herself and refilled her coffee, but this morning she had seen enough of Martha and decided against that second cup. Instead she walked to the reception room, where the biggest fireplace was. She knew Martha kept some of the paper there for setting up the fire. She first listened carefully to ensure Martha wasn't around, and then started inspecting the pile of paper next to the mantel. She was surprised that there was such a large amount of fancy paper that was being used for these invites. It was as though all the well-off families in Roosendaal had kept some spare stationery for when the war was over. Just

so they could start partying again in style. She of all people knew how hard it had been during the war to get good paper. After all, she was the wife of a Royal printer.
At last she found an invite that came from Breda. The envelope had gone missing but the invite itself was pretty clear. August and Louise were invited to come and celebrate the new director of the hat factory in Breda: Jack de Beer. Just reading his name was enough for her to fall into a wonderful and ecstatic daydream. The sole mention of these three small words just made her think of the first time she had met him. At the Liberations Festivities in one of the bars. Louise could not even remember which one. They were all so crowded that they were hard to tell apart. Standing alone with his smile tilting to one side, the same side where his one elbow looked for support on the bar. He did not seem to take in much of the festivities. Instead he was staring at the ceiling, obviously thinking of some place other than where he was standing at that moment. His mates did not seem to mind, as they were preoccupied with the many women who were throwing themselves at them. No one seemed to be interested in this young fellow who stared at the ceiling the entire time. Maybe because of his aloofness or the dreamy look in his eyes. Many may have mistaken that look for a romantic one, but Louise knew better. She had a

radar for men like him. She figured he just wasn't that into these kinds of festivities, and had taught himself to find entertainment in his own head. It had intrigued her right on the spot, but it had not made her go over there. He was the one who initiated their meeting. This move was one of the main reasons she could not understand why he had not kissed her that night. She had revisited that night over and over and over again, but could not for the life of her explain why he would woo her, take her away to a quiet spot to finally reject her. She had never felt so insecure in her life. She had come up with various reasons but none of them seemed viable. He was already married when he approached her. And she had not said anything to put him off. At least she thought not. He had even stroked her hair when he said goodbye. There had been so much chemistry. And not just in her head. She had noticed his chest feverishly moving up and down from breathing harder, and even joked about his urge to bite his lip whenever he looked at her. There was no doubt in her mind that she had an effect on his physic. But the moment she came closer or reached out for his hand, he would back out and keep her at a distance. It seemed as though he was fighting against himself. It made her want him even more, and during the days after their first meeting she could not stop reliving that night in her head. Sometimes she altered the ending and imagined how he would look her in the eyes, tell her that he could not restrain himself any longer, and then finally would find the guts to kiss her. She imagined him backing away for a minute. Just long enough for her to catch her breath. In her mind he turned away briefly, and when she shyly tried to grab his hand he would turn around, pull her tight against his chest and kiss her yet again. He then would take her to a cul-de-sac nearby and push her against a wall, his pained brown eyes piercing through hers. He would softly murmur that he did not know what got into him, and roughly pull her arms above her head. In her dream he was far from handling her with care, and Louise loved it. She imagined him to be passionate and introverted. Her dream would usually end up in him lifting her up and putting her legs around his waist. If she was alone when dreaming of Jack she would sometimes moan softly when she imagined him biting his lip. It usually ended with the realisation of what had really happened.

It hurt her more than it should. She had met this man three times now, and rather platonically, if she was being honest with herself. So why was she so upset? Was it because she was that convinced that her marriage was over? Or was Jack really that special? It was hard to tell sometimes. Louise was a woman born for love, and to state that one love was greater than the other was tricky. Louise only knew how to love in one way: all the way. Many times she had fallen in love and let her fantasies overrule her rational way of thinking. But had it ever hurt like this? Maybe it was the rejection. Louise wasn't really used to being rejected anymore. The last few men she had been with had adored her, kissed the very ground she walked on. And this man, this man knew exactly how to turn her into this adoring, floor-kissing creature. She wondered if he knew this. If he was aware of this effect on her. Probably not to this extent, but surely he must know that he had somewhat of an effect on her? She was never one who needed to look for words, or for her voice for that matter. But of course he did not really know that. He had only met her a few times. So there was no other way for him to find out what he meant to her, than for her to tell him in person. And the party in Breda seemed the only opportunity Louise would have to get him alone. It would become a challenge, to say the least. This celebration was all about Jack, so time would be sparse. And of course Louise would have to take August with her. He had been dying to go to one of the festivities ever since the war had ended, but had not because Louise didn't feel like attending any of them. She couldn't possibly tell him that she would go to a party with Helen and not invite him to go along. Besides, it was frowned upon to attend a party without your husband. So Louise had to come up with a good plan, something she loved to draw up. But first things first. She needed to RSVP to this invite again and write Helen back. Maybe she could ask Helen to help think of a plan for how to get Jack alone. She hastily wrote an RSVP and got upstairs to get dressed. She needed to get out and get some fresh air to think this plan through before she could write back to Helen. As well, there was no way she would let Martha post this RSVP. She would not hear the end of it if Martha would suspect something. When upstairs, Louise finally allowed herself a little giggle. Besides all the planning and the hurt that came with this new love, she was beside herself with joy over this invite. She had not seen him for two weeks now and it had been the longest two weeks she had experienced in years. She knew she was overreacting slightly, but she felt as if her body had just woken up from a winter's sleep. For the first time in years she felt alive again. She felt joy, lust, anger, pain; emotions she had not allowed herself to feel for years. And now they were all back. Without too much warning one man had found a way to finally tear down this wall Louise had carefully fabricated throughout the years. She should be scared, being this exposed. But instead she felt better than ever. Wonderfully free. And that feeling was addictive, she knew. Her vice wasn't liquor. Her vice was love. And as she was softly skipping in her room of joy, she knew that this would not end well. She knew that whatever came from this, someone would end up in pain. And there was not one scenario Louise could think of wherein she would not be one of those pained people. But even that realisation could not alter her mood. She was going to see Jack again!

CHAPTER NINETEEN

The following week was a week of stress. Louise's mood altered every single hour. She went from happily humming tunes to screaming furiously at every object that got in her way. The people around her weren't the least suspicious of her angry episodes. As kind and patient as she was outside of her home, that capricious she was when she was among family. Usually she explained herself to her loved ones by saying that the more she loved someone, the more she felt comfortable in being her true self. August would always jokingly add that she must love him to the moon and back for the way she was herself with him. But she knew that he truly made her a better person, and that she could be so much worse than he could ever imagine.

She proved that yet again to herself in that week before Jack's celebration. She honestly did not understand her own mind sometimes. How could a fairly responsible woman be so hysterical sometimes? When she was in her thirties? Surely other people could not possibly feel this way all the time? And about what really? She thought herself to be a bit childish for panicking for a week on end just because of a party. She was a mother of three for Pete's sake. She had finished grammar school among the best of her class, had survived two world wars and had travelled the world from a very young age. How could she still be so hung up on something as trivial as a love-interest? It frustrated her sometimes. But not as much as it excited her. It was like she needed the drama and the rollercoaster of feelings that came with it. She started to accept that this forever would be the war she would have to fight within her own mind. And she knew which part was winning this battle. Whenever she closed her eyes her mind ran off to the future, where she would see herself laughing and joking in a crowd in a large salon in Breda. She had thought long and hard about her dress. It needed to be an emerald green. A satin version. She had come across a floor-length one with a narrow V-neck and capped sleeves. She already knew she would wear the same colour heels underneath her dress, and fiercely hoped she would not slip this time. Of course the dress would allow her to wear more comfortable shoes, but she could not possibly arrive at a party without heels, now could she? Her bag would be a simple black one. She would pull up her strawberry blonde hair into a loose bun and paint her lips with red. She imagined how he would stare at her when she would be talking to a crowd of people, making them laugh. She would shyly turn her head towards where he would be standing, and she would subtly smile at him. Never in that daydream would she be the first to make contact. She would be mysterious, graceful and charming, and he would not be able to contain himself. And then she thought of something. What if she would be there? What if he were to bring his wife to this event? Not an earth-shaking thought, to bring one's wife to the celebration of your instalment as a director. But then again, wasn't she in the army as well? Did she leave like he did? Or was she still in combat? Louise prayed to God that she still was. All of a sudden she felt sick to her stomach. She really did not want to meet Mrs De Beer. She knew she would behave well and would not give anything away, but the pain it would cause to meet the woman he was spending his days with would be unbearable. Why had it never occurred to her before? Maybe because he never really mentioned her. She did not seem to play a very prominent part in his life. She had to hear from Helen that Jack was married to a woman in the army. Helen had never met her, and it seemed that no one really had. Of course they had gotten married in England, during the war without all his family and friends. But still, if it wasn't for the gossip, Louise would not even know he was married. She decided his wife would simply not attend the event, and tried to focus on creating some alone time between her and Jack. The thought of sharing his attention with another woman that evening simply would be far too stressful for her. And she knew how silly she sounded, but frankly she thought it too much effort to analyse her wondrous mind at this point. She needed all her energy to not lose it before the party next Saturday. Helen had helped her plan the secret rendezvous, but several times the idea seemed a ludicrous plan. How could she ever subtly suggest to him when alone at the bar that they should retire to a place where they could be alone? He was not even willing to let her hand jovially touch his thigh. Why on earth would he follow her into a private place at his own party? But that was the best Helen and Louise could come up with until now. She would dazzle him with her emerald green dress, she would be the belle of the ball and barely look at him. Maybe just once, to subtly exchange an all-knowing smile. She would keep her eyes to the bar and softly ask August if he would like anything to drink the moment she saw Jack approaching the bar. She would smoothly walk towards him, put her purse on the thick wood of the bar and gently curl her fingers in the few strings of hair in the front of her face. She would not look at him at first, would order before him and while waiting on her drinks, would turn her head towards him and smile and simply say hi. He would smile back and ask her how she was. She would cheekily answer: better if you would meet me in five minutes in the bathroom. Lastly she would take her drinks, stride back to her group, hastily down her glass and walk towards the bathroom. He, in awe, would already be there. Five minutes was simply way too long a period for him to wait. Helen thought it waterproof. Louise was still in doubt but no matter how long she racked her brain, there was no other plan that seemed more sensible. She thought of writing him in advance, but she was not sure where he lived these days. And besides, what would she say? No matter how many fantasies she'd had about Jack, nothing had in fact happened. In fact she had tried to put her words on paper several times that week, but it became painfully clear that every assumption she had made about their relationship was indeed that: an assumption. There was no way she could ever write to him what she wanted to write. What if he thought her to be a downright fool? She imagined him reading her letter, shaking his head and not laughing this time. She would definitely cross his line by stating that he had feelings for her. And just a letter about their blooming friendship seemed pointless. If she could look him in his eyes, she would surely know what to say. She was not a shy person, she usually just said whatever she felt to anyone who wanted to listen. But maybe because most of the time she felt she did not have anything to lose. This time she felt she had.

So she recited her plan aloud a couple more times. She reconsidered her dress a few times too, but August was quite set on this dress. He loved her in striking clothing. August was one of those men who loved women who

would dance to their own beat. He did not mind that his wife was often point of interest in many a gossip. He was actually proud of the fact that Louise was one of the most talked-about women in his hometown. She loved that about him. He was secure enough to not let his ambitions overshadow hers. He supported her in every move. And still, he was not enough for her. That pained her, it truly did. But it had been the case for many years now. So the fact that he encouraged her to wear a figure-hugging dress to seduce her love-interest did not even bother her anymore. She had crossed that line so many moons ago, she did not even give it a moment of thought anymore. So she went with August's wish and decided on wearing the green dress. It saved her from stressing about it. All was left to stress about now was how to get Jack alone, and what to say to him. She had practised the words many times out loud. After they would meet each other in the bathroom she would lock the door playfully saying: "We wouldn't want Mrs. Van Dijck powdering her nose in here now would we?" Then she would shyly sigh and look up from underneath her eyelashes to him. She did not plan to be shy, but even in her fantasies she could not bear to look him right in the eye. He had an effect on her like no other man she had ever come across.
"What I wanted to tell you," Louise usually began her speech, "is that…" and then she would usually sigh.

She could not even tell him when he wasn't there, let alone when they were locked in a bathroom together. Just come out and say it, she finally told herself the day of the party when she rehearsed one last time. Just say: "I can't stop thinking about you. Not a moment in the day."
That was all she had planned to tell him. Mainly because she could not come up with anything else, but partly because she really had not the faintest idea of what he would reply. She didn't even know what she wanted him to reply. Every answer would involve a whole lot of pain and or consequences. If he were to like her back, then she would not know how to deal with this situation. She would have to think long and hard over her future. Her future in general and the one with August. Another affair was out of the question, they did not excite her nor revive her marriage. And leaving August? It made her nauseated just thinking about it. If he would tell her she was delusional, then he would have brought to life her biggest nightmare: not being able to tell fantasies and reality apart. And finally, if he would kindly turn her down, she would feel the pain of a perfect gentleman who had turned her down. Either way this night would end up a disaster. So much was certain. Strangely enough this discovery calmed Louise. She could not win or lose, so there was no reason to try either. When she came out

of bed after her midday nap, it immediately hit her: she was really going to see Jack tonight.

CHAPTER TWENTY

The party turned out to be tasteful and thrilling at first. Breda was much more of a city than Roosendaal would ever be. Here, women did in fact wear the latest fashion, not just read about it in women's magazines. She wasn't at all overdressed in her floor-length emerald green gown. Instead she was a little underdressed given the fact that she wasn't covered in jewellery like everyone else. She had contemplated it, getting out the earrings she'd gotten from August on their first anniversary. But it seemed inappropriate to her to already be displaying so much frivolity. She couldn't quite figure out why it bothered her so much, the fact that people just seemed to have forgotten that a few weeks ago they were still at war. It truly baffled her. She understood why Helen, who had friends still waiting for the Germans to leave, tried to forget what had been going on for years. She knew that this was the best way for people to cope with it. Maybe this still applied after the war; to just ignore the reality and go on like nothing really had happened. She in her way was looking for some welcome distraction herself.
However, she refused to look at her feelings for Jack as nothing more than an infatuation. Would an infatuation churn her stomach an entire day? Would puppy love prevent her from eating, thinking straight or even sitting? Surely something so trivial could not have such

a big impact on her daily life. Even now, whilst scanning the crowd for his face, she could not keep her hands from trembling. She decided to not down the wine she was handed a couple of minutes ago. She never knew how she was going to handle her alcohol. And losing control was the last thing she needed right now. Instead she needed to focus and most of all, calm down. But the fact that she still wasn't sure if his wife was going to be there made her even more nervous than she already was. Even August had noticed it. He didn't find it odd that it had taken her ages to get ready, as he already knew her beauty routine could vary from just putting her hair into a bun to spending the entire day curling, bathing and grooming. But he did find it rather alarming that Louise had turned down lunch. She was a healthy eater and was not known to turn down food, especially during the weekends when Martha would usually serve some sandwiches and petit fours, something Louise looked forward to all week. He had asked her if she was falling ill, and had even suggested skipping the party, adding that it might be too soon for her, attending a festivity like that. Louise had panicked a little but knew how to solve this quickly. She knew better than to dispute his theory, so she decided to go with it and alter it to her advantage.
"You're right, dear," she had said softly. "I am nervous of what tonight will bring. It's been such a while since I

have actually gone to a party. Dinners and other gatherings with friends make me feel a lot less nervous. But I need to go. I need to prove to myself that I am returning to my old state again. But forgive me if I come across fidgety or nerve wracked. It's just that I am preparing for tonight to go well. And on that note," she added playfully, "Please watch my drinking if you will? I don't want to make a fool of myself. I am not used to drinking lots of wine anymore."

August had smiled and patted her shoulder. He had kissed his wife and whispered: "you are the belle of the ball, even when you are nervous, tipsy or downright drunk; you're still smarter and funnier than anyone in that room. And I love you for it."

She did realise it sometimes. That the only one who could make her calm enough to get herself together to be able to seduce another man was in fact, her husband. She did see the irony. But then she had already crossed that bridge a hundred other times, and it did not even strike her as odd anymore. She had already discovered that once you cross a line, there is no way back. So she sincerely thanked August for cheering her up, and she continued her bath. By the time they were ready to leave, the nerves had returned. But this time they were so overwhelming she could not even feel her hands anymore. She had felt the blood leave her face in the car when she at last got a grip and prevented herself from getting sick all over her dress. She did not remember being this nervous for a man before. Well maybe when she was still in school and got obsessed with her Latin teacher.

She still wasn't calm after she had drunk her first glass of wine. She had sipped it rather than downed it, and the alcohol seemed to have no effect yet. So much for her plan to entertain a group of men by just being herself. But there was no harm done, yet. She still had not sighted him and she was sure he had not seen her either. She felt vulnerable and foolish, and she found it hard to walk in her heels paired with the floor-length dress. She felt like staying at August's side for the entire time, and crawling into his arms. At least she was safe with him. Meanwhile Helen was having the time of her life. She still needed the distraction of music, other people and alcohol to forget about what was going on. It's funny, Louise thought, how different Helen's merriment felt or how the rest of the crowd seemed to enjoy themselves. Hers truly felt like some much-needed diversion from the pain she had felt the last couple of months, or years really. The others were already used to the warless world, and were already commenting on the dress of Mrs. Sturm, and how she had worn this specific one on numerous occasions already. Everyone knew that they were well-off, so that could not have been the reason of the reoccurring

gown, was the overall consensus. Exactly this kind of talk made it so that Louise would rather spend her time talking to men. Maybe Mrs. Sturm had thought it through and had found it trivial to buy tens of dresses when fabric was still scarce. But of course no one would dare to come up with such a theory. For what on earth would they then talk about? After standing in the corner for almost a quarter of an hour, she decided she needed to get her act together. She decided to walk to the bar to refresh her drink herself, instead of waiting for one of the waiters to do it. She bit through the pain her heels already were giving her, and tried to cross the room as gracefully as her dress would let her. Which was fairly graceful given the circumstances. When she finally reached the bar she grunted softly when she lifted her left foot out of her heel.
"Shoes bothering you already, Marie L? The party hasn't even started yet."
Well of course. That was the first thing he would see when they would finally meet up after weeks of her pining. Louise fought the urge to grab a glass, down it, kick out both her heels and run away. Instead, she laughed, tilted her head, and told him honestly:
"It was the worst decision I have made so far today."
And, of course, that comment invited him to fall into a monologue about how he did not understand why women of her intelligence found it necessary to pain

themselves. He did not understand why society thought it fit to have women struggling to put one foot in front of the other. And he found it even worse that someone like Louise would obey that ridiculous rule. She wanted to cry out and shout: I just think heels are pretty! But she stopped herself and went for a more intelligent approach.
"Let me grab a chair so I can rest my feet during the speech that will no doubt move on to corsets, make-up, and other useless womanly attires."
She stared at him with a fierce look, and hoped to God that he would not see what was beneath that harsh answer. He did not. In fact, he mumbled something and went back to where he'd come from. Louise was left at the bar, and felt the blood drain from her head again. She did down her glass this time, and immediately asked for a refill. She followed Jack through the room and looked to see if she could spot Helen as well. She needed some moral support, quickly. Instead, August suddenly stood next to her and proudly handed her some water.
"You told me I needed to help you cut down the drinking, didn't you darling?" He smiled a kind of victorious smile and watched her drink the glass in one fell swoop. She made the mistake of looking at him whilst drinking, and couldn't help but laugh. He looked so proud for remembering her request. To be honest,

she hadn't expected him to grant her wish. She'd been sure he would forget it as soon as he had his first glass.

"Come darling, just grab my arm. I know you're in pain, I can tell. I'll escort you back to our group."

Louise sighed and put her arm under her husband's, and ignored the burning pain that had formed on the balls of her feet. She kept her eyes on Jack to see if he was watching her. Finally, he looked back at her. She knew it! He was focused on her as well. She shyly turned her head and did not look again until she stood next to Fons and Helen, where August had taken her. Helen signalled to ask everything was going to plan, and Louise responded by sighing dramatically and hitting her head with her hand. That's when Jack passed by and smiled at her. She had gone and done it now. Helen almost sprayed her wine all over Fons, and Fons on his turn switched places with Helen to let the girls talk to each other.

"I've already talked to him," Louise whispered to Helen. "Well, we've spoken to each other", she corrected herself. "He's given me a lecture about wearing heels, and I made him flee by crushing his one attempt to talk to me."

Helen gasped and giggled. It was clear to Louise that her friend had had way too much to drink already. Louise decided to end this conversation before the whole of Breda knew what she was up to. She swiftly left the group, kicked off her shoes, and walked right up to Jack. When he saw her coming he smiled his earth-shattering smile and immediately looked to the floor. He saw her painted toenails peek out of her dress, and chuckled. Before she could reach his party of young men he walked up to her and nodded politely. "I see you have taken off your shoes already Marie L. I am glad I have had the room thoroughly cleaned today."

His brown eyes had a sparkle in them of a brightness that even Louise had never seen before. She covered her left foot with her right foot and forgot all about what she was going to say.

"Maybe you should go back to your husband and let him get some flat shoes for you?"

He sounded sincere. No matter how hard she tried, she could not sense one form of passive aggressiveness in his tone. It shook her to her very core. He had suggested this in the same way Fons would have. There was no trace of hurt or disappointment in his approach. It took a while for her to come up with a response. She did not know if she should still go through with her initial plan to try to talk to him in private.

"I was just wondering if you might have an alternative."

"As in a different pair of shoes?" Jack seemed confused.

"Maybe your mother or wife has the same size shoes as me?" There, this was a legitimate way to find out if his wife had joined him in his move to Breda.

Jack nodded "I see" and left the room in haste. Louise quickly followed him through the doors and ran after him when he climbed up the stairs. She did not know if he wanted her to follow, but this was the perfect way for her to get him alone.

A little room at the back of the house contained some women's shoes. Or at least that was where Jack had led them to.

"Ah, Marie L, you have followed me." His voice sounded distant and harsh, and Louise's courage faded quickly.

"I would not want you to enter the room with a pair of women's shoes, now would I?" she cheerily said.

He mumbled again and started looking through some boxes. She knew she was supposed to ask about his wife now, but she really felt she would not be able to handle anything to do with another woman involved in his life. She thus decided to spring it on him right this moment.

"I can't stop thinking about you," she muttered.

He stopped rumbling but did not turn his face towards her. He kept on facing the boxes, his back in bent in an uncomfortable arch. He then carried on and said nothing. She waited for a few minutes and asked: "What do you think of that?"

He sighed and turned around. After a few paces through the tiny room he decided on sitting on one of the boxes, and looked at her for the first time.

"You're sure it's not just the end of the war? It seems to have stirred up a lot of emotions."

"How can one ever be sure?" Louise responded softly. She sat down next to him and looked him in the eye. Had she really been this wrong about his feelings?

"I guess you can't," he kindly added before he softly slammed his shoulder onto hers.

"I find you extraordinary," he finally added. "But we are both married and there's nothing we can do about that. And besides, you don't want to be thinking about me. I am not as great as you might think."

Louise shook her head, lost for words and probably she had lost her voice too. Her mind was blank. She could only listen to what her body had to say. It had been patient during all the times she had sat and watched his perfect face and body, without coming into action. She felt she could no longer deny her body what it had wanted to do for so long, and so she leaned in for a kiss. She closed her eyes and waited for him to let her lips touch his. When finally she was close to his face she felt his hand on her chest. Right above where her breasts were. He was softly pushing her away from him.

"You don't want to do this, Louise." He did not even use her nickname any longer. "You're really going to regret this."

She looked at him, ashamed, and tried not to scream. Screaming usually was her first reaction when things went terribly wrong; crying never was. She bit her lip, this time not because she was aroused by his handsome appearance, and pleaded with him to stay with her for a little while.

"Marie L…" Ah, there it was again, Louise happily thought.

"We should really be getting back. Come let me help you up."

The thought of going back to the party where August would be and worse, Helen, who would want to know everything, was enough for her stomach to churn yet again this evening. She looked at Jack with panic in her eyes.

"Please stay with me for a few more minutes? I feel mortified. I can't go back in this state!"

"What do you suggest then? They will go looking for us if we don't come back soon, and we will look suspicious. And we're not even doing anything wrong!"

His voice had gone from friendly to panicky, and Louise knew it was time to go. She did not want to put him in a difficult position because of her obvious miscalculations. She stood up, finally, and grabbed the first flat pair of shoes she saw. They were ugly and brown and were a bit too tight. She forced them on her feet and saw Jack already leaving.

"You're not going to wait for me?" Louise couldn't help herself. She usually wasn't this whiny but the pain she felt was unbearable; she did not have any pride left so it seemed.

"Don't you think it's better if we go back separately?"

At least Louise had a true answer for this one.

"Actually no. Only people who have something to hide would do that. We only went looking for shoes."

Jack shrugged and waited for her to put on the brown pair. He then added:

"Marie L, don't be ashamed. It was very brave of you to come out and tell me what you feel, but you must know that I can't help you. You are too late. We're both married and there is nothing we can do about it."

"But weren't you wooing me?" Louise at last asked.

"I might have, and I am sorry about that, Marie L," he answered after a while. "It's a rarity for me to come across someone whom I can be myself with. And whom I find attractive as well. I shouldn't have done so and for that I apologise."

"No, don't!" a relieved Louise blurted out. "I took it to another level without any warning, I must apologise."

"Well, let's try to forget about it, shall we? Let's bring

some life to this party."

CHAPTER TWENTY-ONE

Needless to say, in the end, the party had in no way lived up to the high expectations Louise had set beforehand. When Jack and she had parted their ways, Louise had given up on staying in control and looked for comfort in wine. She drank like there was no tomorrow. The effect of the alcohol at first was a welcoming one. She felt the pain wash away with every sip of wine that reached her stomach. Usually when she drank as much she started dancing or telling everyone how wonderful they were. She was a pleasant drinker who always knew when to stop. This night she did not. She had picked out a spot in a corner and had the waiter serve her wine as soon as her glass was empty. The more empty wineglasses the waiter picked up, the emptier her stare became. She stood there, in her corner, for hours on end it seemed, just mumbling away. When anyone would pass by her she would inaudibly mumble something the likes of: "Watch out, I might mistakenly think you like me," and then wave them off in a rude manner. August had come to check up on her and she had begged him to take her home. But August did not ever want to go home. Once he was at a party, he was definitely among the people who would leave last. Too busy with having too much fun himself, he scattered off and left Louise alone in her drunken state. She cringed the next morning when she thought back of when Jack had passed by and asked her if everything was all right. She had turned her head and grunted that he should not pay any attention to her, in case she would again think he was coming on to her when clearly he was not. She hit her already-sore head with her hand and let out a soft cry of despair. She could not remember the last time she had felt this bad. It was as though a train had run over her, backed up and run over her again. Her body felt beaten, her head pounded and her heart... O her heart. Usually she could find relief in the slightest gestures or words. But she could not find anything in his voice, words or manners that could soften the blow. She went through the night over and over again, but there was no way out, she had to face it: her pursuit of Jack was at a dead end. Yes he had been kind, but he had pushed her away. No matter how gently he had done it, she, Marie Louise, had been pushed away. She had opened up completely, torn down every stone of her wall and was her most vulnerable when he had put his hand on her chest and pushed her back to reality. She could still feel his cold hand on her skin.

She pulled her blankets up to her eyes and squinted. Surely now some tears would flow? What was wrong with her? Ever since she was a little girl she hadn't been able to cry. She wondered why. All she ever heard was that women cried all the time. By the sight of a puppy, a sad story in a woman's magazine. She on the other hand could only cry when she went to the pictures by herself. When she was alone in the dark and would let the massive images of the theatre in, she could sometimes cry silently. For nothing in particular usually. Tears would just cover her face, and her mouth would dry from being open the entire time. She sometimes went to a matinee by herself to let some emotions out, for no reason. Of course the fact Louise went to the pictures by herself was a source for even more gossip. What woman would go see the movies by herself in the afternoon? Someone rich for one, and a woman with no good intentions, surely. Louise couldn't be bothered. She continued going and felt relieved when she would leave the theatre with red eyes and a swollen nose. She contemplated going today but then realised it was Sunday. She immediately got up and held on to her headboard, the alcohol still had a grip on her. She put on her dressing gown and walked downstairs. The house seemed empty. No children who ran around, nothing on the stove, no deafening Wagner that drowned out every thought. She had complained about this every single time August had put on this German composer. Wagner had been associated with Hitler and it hardly seemed appropriate to blast out his music. Especially not on a Sunday, the day of God of all days. But this morning all was silent. Louise walked on to the kitchen and put on the kettle. She finally looked at the clock and suddenly understood why everyone seemed to be out. It was already noon, which meant she had missed Mass. Not even when you are sick are you allowed to miss Mass! Even during her time in bed after Gus and Frank, she still had to go to church on Sundays. She panicked. Why on earth would August have let her sleep? Was he upset? What had she done? She ran upstairs, ignoring the fact that her brain seemed to travel loosely in her head. She quickly took off her bath rope and night gown, and rinsed her body so the smell of alcohol wouldn't be as predominate. She then ran downstairs in a hurry, for she heard the kettle whistle. She turned off her AGA stove and ran back upstairs to get dressed. When she was halfway up she stopped and heard the front door open. She was naked and needed to get upstairs before anyone would see her. She heard Gus screaming that he was hungry, and chuckled when she heard Betty correct him. For a moment she thought of crawling back into bed, but decided to face the music instead and quickly put on a dress. When she entered the reception room, the house was lively and energetic again. There was no room for her thoughts anymore.

CHAPTER TWENTY-TWO

For some reason the kitchen always had a soothing effect on her. Whenever Louise felt stressed or frustrated, she yearned for her kitchen. Just the thought of getting her hands into a ball of dough or dicing up a load of vegetables for her world-famous soup made her breathing steadier. Louise was a good cook, always on the hunt for an exotic recipe. She was the first in her circle to use chutney as a side to her dishes. In the Netherlands, no one had ever tasted such a foreign and spicy substance. And while – secretly – even Louise at first did not care for the strong aftertaste at all, after a few dinner parties, people actually started to request her chutney. It was the art of creating something that was in some way unique, with her own hands and mind that made her love being in her kitchen. That, and the fact it was her absolute dream kitchen. Complete with the AGA stove and lots of storage. Louise wasn't the only woman in her circle to have a state-of-the-art kitchen. She was, however, the only one who would actually use it. Most households employed a cook or a maid with great cooking skills. And yes, their maid of course whipped up the regular meals, but when Louise felt the way she felt today, Martha was dismissed.

When she entered the kitchen she ran her hands over her AGA. Her father-in-law had bought her this beauty with her husband's money She grabbed the handles, looked up to the ceiling and breathed out very slowly. She tried to breathe out all the anger, frustration, pain and despair. But there were too many emotions for one single sigh. Her throat started to swell up and she tried to swallow away the painful chunk of sorrow that seemed to be stuck there. At once she straightened her shoulders and started pulling open her cabinet doors. She hadn't planned to cook tonight, so she had no idea what to make. She felt like pie, something comforting and soothing.

Her hands seemed to need no help from her brain while getting the ingredients. Mindlessly they gathered the eggs, flour and butter. He would never guess she could be this calm, this quiet and in pain, she muttered to herself while folding the dough around the slices of butter. He thought he knew her so well. That there was no trait she could hide from him, no emotion that would slip his attention, but he must be wrong. There was no way Jack knew her better than she knew herself. She refused to accept it. But it had troubled her lately. The woman he had described when talking about her, she recognized somehow. Like a once beloved aunt or cousin whom she had lost touch with along the way. The Louise he saw wasn't the responsible, all-knowing housewife who people came to for advice. He saw a vulnerable, intelligent, creative woman who was clumsy and above all, very loving. And it did not matter how much she tried to convince him she was confident and put together, he stood his ground. If she was being honest, trying to convince him had only made matters worse. She had the tendency to turn into a helpless child when around him. So it's not that this image Jack had of her, had surprised her much. What did surprise her is how badly she had wanted to be that person. In his presence her answer was just an opinion, not a direction or decision. There was no fear of not knowing something, for it would only mean that she lacked some knowledge. Not that there was no solution to a problem. It is not fair stating that at home she was omniscient, that August knew nothing. August was as intelligent as she was. But when it came to life, he knew less than an impatient child starting school: eager to learn, but too excited to actually absorb something.

She loathed and yet loved the way she felt around Jack. Louise had worked hard to be this strong and fairly independent woman. She prided herself on running her life the way she did. And yet, it felt like home to let go of that armour and just be herself. With Jack there was no way she felt scared or lost. She felt like a protected child, loved by both her parents. For a short while. Because the moment she would let her guard down entirely and let herself float in this pool of comfortable homelike feelings, Jack would pull the plug. All of a sudden she would be drenched and cold and exposed

to the world. Her feelings were misplaced. He made her feel safe, but with him she was anything but. He would never choose to spend his life, or even a portion of it, with her. And although he could not let her be, he could not stop interfering with her life, her feelings or emotions, there was just no way he would ever see himself with Louise.
It had turned her into a bitter woman. There had never been anyone before Jack who had paid so much attention to her. Who had put so much effort into getting to know her. But no matter how much he seemed to be invested in her welfare, he claimed to have no feelings at all. Not only for Louise. Jack actually prided himself on being a rational human being. And the last thing he craved for was an emotional, sometimes even hysterical woman who drove his emotions to the surface. So close to the surface even, that sometimes his rational brain was powerless. There was no feeling in the world he hated more, he had told her once. The lack of control when near her. To Louise it was the ultimate proof that his feelings were just as strong as hers. But it did not matter. Jack did not budge, and Louise was left in pieces, every single time they parted.

She startled when Martha came in asking if she needed any help, surprised to see her hand aggressive kneading the dough for her chicken and leek pie. She was planning on making a puff pastry, which needed to be folded. Confused, she held the ball of dough in her hand and blew a string of hair out of her face.

"You're not going to throw it at me, are you, Louise?" Martha looked genuinely scared.

It pained Louise to have this relationship with Martha, as they used to get along so well. Ashamed, she lowered her arm and rolled the ball back into the bowl.

"Of course not, you daft woman." For some reason she could not find the strength to make the first move to rekindle their friendship.

"I was just wondering what to do with it, it's too solid for a puff pastry."

Martha shrugged her shoulders and decided upon leaving the kitchen instead of offering any help. She was weird like that sometimes. As if miss manners had urged her to ask the polite question, and her own reasoning took over during the good deed. Louise was used to this behaviour but was still not sure as to what to do with her dough.

She decided to start anew. A rare choice, but she needed to prove to herself that she could for once finish what she had started. Something Jack doubted she was capable of.

As she started to fold the newly made dough around the butter, she got angrier and angrier. Without him in the room she could see so much more clearly. It was time he came off his high horse and started looking at his own actions. For in words yes, he had never led her on. Never. But as actions go, he was not as innocent as he was all too happy to portray. After the party she had retreated, licked her wounds and concluded that she had to let him go. No more scheming, no more volunteering at the hospital. She needed it to get through to her that she had a husband and three children, and that pursuing another man who had been very clear about his intentions would not at all be a desirable path. After all, she was about to turn 35 years this summer, and it was time to grow up, she had told herself.

It was Jack. Jack who had stood at her front door in the middle of the afternoon. Jack who had come in and who had ignored her shocked face. It was he who had been pacing around this very kitchen, intensely inspecting her foreign appliances and lovingly sighing every time he had found something that was 'typically Louise'.

After the initial shock, panic started entering Louise's body. What was he doing here? She searched frantically for a clock, and checked to see if Martha or the children were expected back anytime soon.

"Don't worry about your family, Louise. I know they will not be back for at least an hour; I did my homework."

Louise, not a stranger to obsessive research, did not seem bothered by this somewhat off-putting remark back then. But at this moment, while she was roughly deboning a chicken, she scowled at this clear sign of equal obsession. He had bothered to find out when her children would get out of school! She screamed inwardly.

When Jack was done inspecting her kitchen, he found himself a chair and expected her to sit down too. Not sure whether to sit next to him or maybe opposite him, she chose a chair that was already pulled away from under the table. It turned out to be much too close to him, as she immediately smelled him. Like clockwork her body started to relax, and her lungs seemed to fill themselves with much-needed air. She lowered her shoulders and felt her voice had come back:

"Let's first make you some tea."

She remembered not waiting for his answer, but walking straight to the cupboards she was standing in front of right now, looking for a little bowl to crack some eggs in.

Before he could start his monologue, which she was sure was coming, she started to loudly look for some cups and saucers. She put on the kettle and went on looking for that tea she had been keen to try out.

"Louise, please sit down."

Reluctantly she obeyed his wish and chose a chair farther away. She laid her hands on her table and folded them together; they seemed to want to reach for his like they were magnetic.

"I want to know how you are doing."

A shiver entered her spine as she was brushing the egg onto her chicken and leek pie. She had to think of another dish to make, for it was obvious that there was still a lot of thinking to be done. He seemed sincere that day, Louise decided. But then again she could not for the world think of any sound reason why he would come all the way to Roosendaal, find out when she was alone and invite himself into her kitchen, just to find out if she was all right. But at that very moment, her brain was clearly out of order.

"Fine, fine. I am totally fine." She attempted to get up so she could go on with the business of making tea to fight off the nausea, when he grabbed her hand and softly forced her to sit back down again.

"Are you really? I have been worried about you ever since the party."

This time Louise had to get up. The kettle had started to whistle, softly at first so they were still able to ignore it, but inevitably the whistle became nothing short of a scream and Jack had to let go of Louise's hand.

Moving on to dessert, Louise could still feel his hand on hers. He was the type of person who had to live with cold limbs throughout the year. She on the other hand was warm-blooded all the bloody time. Her hands would usually be warm, almost hot even, and feeling rather greasy no matter how many times she would wash them. She was insecure about this and was rather happy that Jack had put his on top of hers, as at least he could not comment on the backs of her hands.

When she came back, Jack had found his old confidence he usually displayed when he was alone with her. She had felt the mood shift when she poured the water into the teapot and looked for biscuits to go with the tea. Instead of sitting straight and tightening his muscly arms, Jack had positioned his body into a more familiar state. When she walked over to the table concentrating on the large tray, keen on not spilling anything this time, she noticed his shoulders to be so much relaxed. Which meant with him, they were facing downwards.

"Why would you want to know how I am feeling, Jack?"

She tried overpowering his relaxed state by using a stern tone.

"Because of what you tried to do at the party, Louise. That must have had some effect on you."

"Well, let's try and relive it then, shall we? Let's analyse what silly old Louise did to you and go about it step-by-step. You're right, that ought to cheer me up! Boy, you do know me like no other."

She wondered why she only had two sorts of replies when in his presence. Either she was being the shy and silent girl, or she was on some kind of path to war. Which she was on now, obviously.

Jack, never scared of a reply, immediately raised his voice.

"I know you are scared to hear what I have to tell you. But you need to really hear it. I do not have the same feelings. You mean a lot to me, but I am not in love with you."

He stared right into her eyes. She was glad that she was sitting down, for it felt that the floor had just fallen out from under her feet. It's not like she did not expect him to say these words. She had suspected it the minute he entered her kitchen, but his words still seemed to feel like a fatal blow to the head.

"Well luckily you came all the way over here to tell me this yet again. At least I have someone who cares for me here, to soothe the pain."

They had talked to each other in this manner ever since they had met each other. The few talks on the bench near the hospital had deepened their strange bond, and after a few weeks they already sounded like husband and wife.

"But I am guessing that you are not here to put a comforting arm around me, now are you, because that would mean that you would have to touch me. And isn't that cheating in your book?" Louise cringed as she remembered what came next.

"You know what, you have got a lot of nerve, coming here and inviting yourself in just to hurt me even more. You were quite clear back at the party, and you might remember that since then I have not tried to contact you or see you. So why did you think you coming over here was a good idea? God must know, because I for one am at a huge loss. So if you do not mind, Jack. Get the hell out of my kitchen."

Anyone else would have been stunned or hurt or affected in some way. But Jack had merely stood up and just looked at her smiling.

"My poor monkey, don't get so wound up. I just

wanted to help you get over me. Come and sit next to me and drink your tea, it will all be all right."

His voice soothed Louise and she went back to the chair somewhat to close to him. She smelled his scent again and felt all anger leave her body. Without thinking she laid her head against his shoulders. Well at least she tried.

The thought of his reaction made her drop the net of oranges she had just grabbed from the pantry. When she got onto the floor to pick them all up, she cringed all over again.

Before her head landed on his bony shoulders he had stood up again in a hurry and lost all reason.

"Haven't I been perfectly clear about this, Louise? This is never going to happen. You can try and lay your head anywhere you want and try and seduce me, but I will stand my ground. How dare you not listen to what I just have been saying?"

He grunted and started pacing through the kitchen. It was Louise's turn to be touched. She could not help it but smile. Of course at first she felt incredibly ashamed that he had yet again rejected her, but this reaction displayed so much despair. It was not a reaction of someone who did not care.

"I was just looking for some friendly support, that was why you came to tell me this yourself, right? Don't be such an incredible baby, sit down and drink your tea."
She kept on surprising herself with her replies. It seemed as though her mouth and her mind led completely different lives. Her mouth was quick and sharp as soon as her voice was available. Yet her mind was in all kinds of panic states whenever Jack's scent entered her nostrils. It just did not work in his presence. Hours after he left it had started to work again. But it wasn't until today, more than a week later, that Louise had really started to think over Jack's impromptu visit.

He must love me too, she eagerly concluded.

CHAPTER TWENTY-THREE

For the first time in years, Louise had been able to throw a Christmas dinner for her family again. Mainly because the war had ended, but more importantly because she felt more of a woman, a wife and a mother than in the four dark years before. Jack had brought life into her bones again and had given her the strength to fight for her marriage and children. She no longer was amazed by this paradox, for she had come to terms with this somewhat cruel irony. The irony of needing someone apart from her husband to help her believe in the life she had led for 10 years now. Merrily she had gone to the attic to find her old cookbooks again, and was delighted to find some recipes that did not need any exotic ingredients. Food was still rather scarce, but because of her husband's network she had been able to buy the few groceries she did need for an extraordinary feast. Little Frank was too small to enjoy any of her cooking, but Gus and even picky Betty stuffed their mouths with all the delicious courses she had made from scratch. Usually surrounded by friends and family, this Christmas August and Louise had decided against inviting anyone. Both had silently agreed upon an intimate family dinner, for it seemed the only way to rekindle what was once a good and steady marriage. As an exception Louise had even shared her dinner plans with August, so he could provide the right wines with the different courses. Little Gus had shrieked with pleasure when he found out he was allowed to drink some of his father's fancy wine. The thrill of joining the grown-ups soon subsided when he tasted his first glass of wine, for he found it 'ghastly'. Louise and August cried tears of laughter when their eldest son had uttered the posh word after spitting out every last drop of red wine. He seemed happy to go back to the grape juice his little sister and brother were drinking, and swore he would never drink again. All in all, Louise enjoyed this little display of family bliss. Her vow to leave August for good felt overdramatic, and she decided to store away the thought next to the traumas of war. She had already given up on leaving right after she found out she was carrying Frank, but she had not done so voluntarily. This Christmas she seemed to have found peace in the idea of spending the rest of her life with August and their three children. Looking at them from a distance while she was finishing up the dessert made her feel a true mother again, a feeling so foreign to her for so long. She did worry about her bond with little Frank though. He did not seem to connect with her at all. That thought made her weary and threatened her newfound mood.

To cheer herself up, her mind immediately sprang to default mode: Jack. But the mere thought of him was enough for her to fall into a deep misery. The dinner she had made, the loving words she aimed at her husband, the letting go of the thoughts of leaving August. How could she have thought that a simple dinner would fix all the problems she and August were having? She started to whisk her cream more aggressively by the minute, angry with herself for allowing herself to believe in fairy tales. This family was beyond salvation, it was founded on deceit and held onto nothing more than determining circumstances. She threw her whisk into the sink and wiped her forehead with her hands. Her mood had shifted within seconds, and all of a sudden she detested the wine August had picked out for her. She did not want this simple life where she had to take care of her own happiness. She wanted someone besides herself to make her happy for once. And somehow she thought Jack was the one person up for the job. After she had ladled the whipped cream over the freshly baked apples, she returned to the dinner table and tried to hide the enormous shift in her mood. But August was no fool, she knew, and saw immediately what was wrong. He too had believed for a short while that their family was safe from her adamant obsession with change. When she had come back from the kitchen, August had known his thoughts had been in vain. He poured another glass without refilling hers. She knew then and there that he too had given up.

~

Putting up the Christmas tree and taking it down again. A tradition Marie Louise cherished like no other. Chores like laundry and dusting were passed onto her maids, but every year she insisted on taking down the tree herself. She loved all the Christmas ornaments she had collected over the years. Each piece contained a different memory. It soothed her, the hours of decluttering her home. It usually gave her some sense of normalcy. Just one of those rare moments she was content with being a housewife. For once she would not feel the wrath of domestic imprisonment. Carefully she would pack and stow away each ornament while listening to Bing Crosby and Perry Como. But this year, not even this tradition could soothe her pain. For she started to realize that next year she might not be having this ritual at this time. What if this feeling would not go away? What if this situation would get worse? Ever since last Christmas dinner she had not been able to shake off these thoughts. The beginning of the end was starting to dawn on her. There had always been a way back. There had always been some sort of hope that everything would just resolve itself. That her feelings were hormonal, that they would subside and she would see clearly again. She always had that glimmer of hope that her life would stay the way it had been for the last couple of years. That she would not be such a selfish person. That she would find the strength to stay for her family, her children, her husband. Others seemed to be strong enough. Why should that not be her? According to her friends, Marie Louise was a loving and caring and selfless person. A stable and wise woman with light-hearted wits about her. Yes, she was someone who embraced life and sometimes touched the borders of what one should or should not do in the society she lived in. But she was always granted the benefit of the doubt. She hated that image of her, and knew that if she would ever meet anyone like herself, she would immediately loathe that person. Not because that person would turn out to be a fake, but because she knew that person would not have the guts to show his or her faults. If she had been able to confess her imperfections the proper way, she might not have been in this mess. For she realized it all too well, that January in 1946. There was no way back now. Although nothing had been damaged beyond repair and her marriage could still be amateurishly taped together, she knew her heart and obsessive mind would not let go. She would go on until everything she held dear would burn right in front of her eyes, and the eyes of her loved ones. There was no other way out. She carefully rolled every bauble and adornment in old newspapers her husband printed every single day, and she took one last look at each of them. She silently bid them goodbye. The ballet dancer she got in Vienna, the antique baubles she inherited from her favourite aunt, and the adornments she got in London right before the war broke out. She did not know exactly when she would close her door behind her indefinitely, but she knew it would be before another Christmas would arrive. What her life would look like, she had no idea of. It scared her more than it gave her adventurous heart joy. For she knew now that these feelings did not have anything to do with her youth. They were not hormonal or temporary. They were part of her character. It was not something she could accept easily. A novelty, for Marie Louise never regretted anything that made her long for adventure. Life was for learning from mistakes, and imperfections were perfect to learn from. But next to her destructive traits lay her more caring character. Her ability to love like no other. Her softer and selfless side. All was overshadowed by this need for destruction. So for once she did not shake her shoulders and say: such is life. She suffered in silence. So she poured herself a glass of wine. A glass of wine without the company of others – that too was a new experience. Marie Louise loved to drink, but she was a social drinker. She did not crave for alcohol when she was alone like so many others. But now she found the bottle rather numbing. After a drink or three she did not feel as confused and, frankly, evil. She was not sure she could ever love herself again the way she used to. She always advised her friends to love themselves, for she thought it the reason of her wonderful life.

"If you love yourself," she would often brag, "someone else will see what you see and love you even more, for it is always easier to love someone else."

Alcohol provided her with a soft shell around her harsh thoughts of herself. It would pause her destructive feelings and let her laugh again. So that night she opened a second bottle to numb the revelations she had experienced under the tree. She had chosen a red wine. Her husband had numerous wines of various, mainly high, prices and red seemed to match her mood. The weariness the red wine provided felt soothing and necessary for her to get some sleep later on. Sleep always came easily. As soon as she closed her eyes, sleep would come. But her dreams were more violent these last few weeks. Sleep did not rest her anymore. She became more and more reluctant to go to bed. Waking up next to her husband was just one of the reasons. She used to love seeing his calming face the moment she woke up. But nowadays she only saw the face she was eventually going to leave. And why? She would never be able to explain. She could not even explain it to herself. She loved him, he was her rock, her everything. Her family loved him. Everyone did and rightly so. He was a wonderful man. But she did not appreciate him enough anymore. That hurt her more than anything else. She truly wished him a better wife, a better life. She sometimes was horrible to him. Every little fault he had she magnified and exaggerated. She sometimes even humiliated him in public. She was not that kind of person. She hated the way she was around him lately. The man who had done everything to make her happy. The only person ever who understood her vaguely, the only person who had bothered to look underneath the surface.

But he still saw her as a better person than she actually was. No one saw the enormous flaws in her character. Even when she told people about them. There was no way that angelic Marie Louise was that bitter, that evil, and that selfish. There was just no way. She took another sip of her red wine. She had no idea what kind she was drinking. Sometimes it interested her, the art of drinking wine. But on this night she just could not care less. She was pleased with this pick though. The soft filter it left behind was comparable to the soft shell that started to form around her thoughts. Slowly but steadily her thoughts lost their sharpness. Her feelings muted and her stomach finally stopped turning. Instead, there was a sharp pain in her abdomen. A sour fluid started to rise to her gullet. A welcome diversion from the nauseating feeling she underwent every single day for months. She poured herself another glass, turned up the radio and closed her eyes. His face filled the room immediately. Within seconds, she imagined his lips near hers, his pained eyes piercing through hers. She almost felt his slender fingers against her cheek. And then suddenly she opened her eyes and remembered his rejection. His soft push when she tried to kiss him. He had admitted he felt the same, but was not willing to let both of them break their vows. He gently pushed her away and asked her to leave. She cringed when she thought back to that night at his party, when she had refused to obey that wish. When she'd begged him not to reject her, not to ask her to leave but to hold her and stroke her hair so she would not feel so alone. Most of the time Marie Louise pretended that night did not happen. That there was never a night she had made such a fool of herself. But obviously, she could not forget. And she had found comfort in the fact that he had not found it desperate, but loving and cute. That he still had a weak spot for her, maybe even loved her judging by his coming over to talk it through. But that he was an honest man. A man who would never betray his wife and let someone else betray her husband. But that he too was tempted. And that if he would ever, that she definitely would be the one. It had provided some sort of hope. Some sort of salvation. But a part of her was scared of this little window. For she knew that she would always get her way. That was no arrogance of hers. She sometimes wished it were. She just knew what she was capable of. And he did not. He did seem like an honest man. And she wondered why she would never fall for types like herself. The adventurous and limitless men. She always went for the good ones. The straight ones. She hated herself for that. She would ruin these wonderful men for life, and no other woman would ever experience the good these men had in them. She comforted herself with the thought that she might just be what these men were looking for. But she never really embraced this theory. When she had almost finished her second bottle, she could not really feel her fingers anymore. She was not used to this excessive drinking of hers. It frightened her. The loneliness had reached a new low point. There was no one left who would understand. Who would still her destructive thoughts? The only person who came close was the one person she would hurt the most. She still had the clearness of mind to clear away the empty bottles of wine and the used, crystal glass. Hurt and disillusioned Marie Louise climbed her stairs and undressed slowly. She knew she would fall down if she did not undress carefully. When she had finally found her night gown, she heard the door open. She knew August was home. Swiftly she went to bed and closed her eyes. Tears formed at the corners of her eyes. Fortunately it did not take more t

t

han a minute before sleep came and took her away to a restless dream world.

CHAPTER TWENTY-FOUR

His hand accidentally touched Louise's palm. A shiver went through her spine. She was never keen on being touched. Which didn't quite match her personality. Louise was known for her warm approach. She usually soothed nervous company by lightly touching their shoulders or softly patting their arm. But when she was the one being comforted thusly she would often clench her teeth. She was incredibly private when it came to her skin. But the mark Jack had left with his index finger was a welcome one. Her body tensed, and Louise wondered if he could see the goose bumps that had appeared around her neck and arms. Her left hand softly caressed the skin in between her right thumb and index finger. He had said something to her while touching her, but she had been temporarily deaf. After swallowing away the intense response on his touch, she huskily asked him to repeat his sentence.

"You should take your automobile to the auto shop, Louise. The engine should not be making such a rattling noise." To emphasise his words he added a grunting sound by scraping his throat.

His face was stern like it always was when he told her off. It seemed to be a hobby of his, pointing out her little faults. It kept on surprising her, this hold he had on her. She was an independent woman, known for her strength and responsibility. She was the sort of person people came to for advice. She had her driver's license, a rarity for a woman, handled her household's finances, she had a university degree and a flying license for Pete's sake. But in his company she was 13 years old again, obeying her father and waiting for his confirmation. To others Jack was an odd and sweet man. Not a dominant creature or someone to fear. But she craved his approval and always seemed to miss some detail in his presence. And fighting this role he put her in made no difference. In fact, it made things worse. His face then would break out into this bright smile and cause a fog to enter her mind, making it impossible to reply anything else than a chuckled 'sorry'.

She looked up at his brown eyes framed by his bushy eyebrows, and stared at the wrinkles in between. He looked so serious, it made her smile. She couldn't help but burst out in laughter. Tears ran over her cheeks when she saw his stern face transform to a question mark.

'I am serious, Marie L, this car is a hazard. I really don't understand why you think your lack of safety is a joke.'

Nervously he scratched his cheek, and the sound his nails made on his stubble took away all the laughter. She studied the dark hairs on his face and focused on the birthmark near his ear. She swallowed again and imagined how his beard would rub her chin when kissing her chin and neck. Hastily Louise turned her face away and glanced at his bony ankles, scarcely exposed underneath his khaki trousers. He had an odd taste in clothing. Although slightly younger than Louise, Jack tended to dress like a retired professor. She kind of thought it to be a cute look. But it didn't suit him much. Most of the time he was dressed in shades that drowned all the colour out of his face. He was already incredibly pale, but the often-light tints of his shirts and trousers turned him into a ghostlike figure.

She had pointed it out once, this mismatch in colour and his skin. And she instantly regretted it. For starters, she loved the way he dressed. He stood out in a crowd. And not for being flashy or flamboyant. But for being understated and different. And so what that the beige trousers made him look somewhat pale and lost. She loved him for it. And now she had to watch him defend himself in an insecure way. She knew she had gotten to him. She got to him like many other times before. And she always regretted it afterwards. She knew why she did it. She knew why it was so incredibly hard to stay open and honest with this man who could so easily hurt her. It was exactly that reason that made her vile and mean sometimes.

Louise was not an emotional woman. Although a great supporter of dramatic situations, gestures and people, crying about it in public was not her style. And even if it was, she couldn't. Louise could not cry when not alone. Ever. Her father thought it to be her best trait: "You hold up your emotions like a man," he would say. "That'll take you far in life."

She agreed with him up to a point. But sometimes she wished she could. For it felt like all the tears that should be hiding behind her eyes would have to come out eventually. That somewhere at the back of her head there was a solid bank, holding back years' worth of salty water. It would explain her excruciating headaches. But her face stayed dry. Even now, with her marriage in ruins, her constant struggle to put her children first and the constant rejections of Jack, Louise hadn't been able to shed a single tear.

Instead, she chose to protect herself from more harm by lashing out before someone else could lash out at her. And the one who had been lashing out the most was Jack. By rejecting her over and over again. But it wasn't even the lashing out, Louise tried to protect herself from. It was his genuine interest in who she was, that had hurt her the most. It didn't make sense to her. His worries about her car. Even August, who was very keen on keeping her alive, did not care as much. Jack seemed to interfere with everything she did. But with no other intention than to be her friend. And even maintaining a friendship with her did not seem to be his top priority. So was it his overall kindness? Was he

like this to everyone? She knew for sure he wasn't.
For starters he had basically proposed to go for a drive after they had left Fons and Helen's new year's get together, as they called it. She had only suggested taking him home. But as so often they had not been able to say goodbye to each other just yet. He had then offered to treat her to some afternoon tea, which she had politely refused. She was not up for another hour of sitting in an uncomfortable silence, waiting for him to determine the topics to discuss. Whenever she would start talking about subjects that interested her, politics, literature or the general news, he would stop her and add that he did not care for small talk.
"That is what draws me to Wendy." He exaggerated the e of Wendy and looked straight at Louise.
No matter how obvious his intentions were, hearing the name of his wife made her wish she was giving birth again instead.
"She never tries to fill the silence with whatever nonsense that comes to mind."
"Wendy does not have a degree, I presume."
Louise's first reaction would always be a vile one.
"I mean, I sometimes tend to forget that people who did not attend University do not care much for literature or politics."
It was so unlike her to put herself above people who did not have as much schooling as she had had. There

were few people Louise did not find interesting, no matter what their education level was.

"Did anyone ever tell you that you are a true snob?"

They would continue to offend each other and their loved ones until someone would have the guts to get up and leave.

At any cost Louise had wanted to avoid another falling out. So when it became clear that he would not get out of the car, she suggested they could go for a drive. He had agreed instantly but had made it sound as though he would be doing her a huge favour. She did not mind, for she was happy not to depart from him just yet. Louise was an incredibly fast learner, but when it came to Jack she made the same mistakes every single time they were together. Days before their rendezvous she would imagine how he would finally admit his feelings for her, and she would again sink further into her fantasies. Daydreams in which he would finally put his words into actions. Because although he had never touched anything besides her hand or cheek, he had described on numerous occasions what he would do to her when he would have the chance. In fact he had had the chance before, but he had always chickened out or proclaimed that he was never serious about these intimate intentions. But no matter how many times he had physically pushed her away, or had pleaded that he had no feelings for her whatsoever, she had always held hope. Hope that one day he would forget about his wife and his doubts, and lose control over his body and devour hers because of it.

But like all others, this encounter did not bring the release she so longed for. After his bugging her about her engine and driving skills, she got fed up and drove him back to his home. As she pulled up his driveway he started fiddling with the door handle already. He seemed eager to get out. Tired of his fear of touching her, she then bent over him and brushed her breast against his lap, and opened the door of the passenger side where he was sitting. When she returned to her own seat she looked him deep into his eyes and whispered goodnight. He shivered and seemed frozen in his seat. She adjusted her mirror and bit her lip. She knew she came across cool and collective, but she in fact was holding her breath. She wanted him to leave as soon as possible so that she could scream in the privacy of her car. Maybe even light a cigarette, something she almost never did. She felt Jack coming back to his senses, and she started reapplying her lipstick to distract herself. Her body tensed when Jack threw the door shut, and without giving so much as a glance she drove away. After a few meters she stopped her car again and looked for a cigarette in the glove compartment. Screaming was not an option right now. She nervously lit her cigarette, wondering what brand it was. A mind was a miraculous place, she thought. How could her mind be wondering about something that trivial when in fact her entire body was ready to basically give up on life. She looked at the package and read 'Gauloise'. When the smoke reached her lungs, she felt her body relax and she threw the package back into the glove department. Better luck next time, she sighed and started up her car again. It sprang to life immediately. You see? She thought. There is nothing wrong with my engine.

CHAPTER TWENTY-FIVE

Even August had had enough of Louise's unstable moods, she suspected. They had found a kind of rhythm both parties seemed reasonably okay with. In between her meetings with Jack, Louise had been her depressed self and had retreated an awful lot to her room next to Gus'. But at least neither of them seemed to feel that the end was inevitable anymore. Come spring, they actually started talking again. Louise wasn't sure if they were in fact on their way up, or if it was just easier to pretend. She and Jack had been seeing each other quite regularly, providing her with the energy to pretend her life wasn't in complete shambles. To her, getting out of bed every single morning and putting up a brave face for her children was more than she could have ever thought to accomplish after the decision she had silently made about her life multiple times. And although Jack had distracted her from her plan to leave August a couple of times, she still was set on forming a plan. To be honest, most of the time she did not feel energetic enough to even think about leaving, let alone think up a plan. And the times she did feel kind of happy was when she was with Jack. So she had resigned herself to a routine of getting to bed right after dinner with a novel, and sleeping for at least 12 hours straight every day.

When she walked up the stairs for yet another early

night, August called after her.

"Maybe we should go away. Just the two of us. It'll do both of us some good. After all, we haven't been away for years, and I can't wait to make some miles with the car again."

She softly chuckled. Although August loved driving, there was no way you could call him a solid driver. Neither was she, but he seemed to forget the trouble he got in every time he got behind a steering wheel.

"Don't you reckon, my love? Just you and me in a car for hours? Remember Italy?"

She did remember and smiled at no one, still frozen on the stairs. For some reason there was no reply to be found in this gloomy head of hers.

August decided to walk towards the stairs, wondering if he had been too late and Louise was already in bed. He was the only one beside her to still be awake at this hour, but even had he not been, Louise would have recognised his footsteps in a heartbeat. Although not very heavy or incredibly tall, August walked like a giant. For some reason he always landed his feet as though they were searching for sturdy ground in a deep swamp. The sound the soles of his shoes made on the hard floorboards would echo through the entire house, and it never occurred to him to take off his shoes. When he entered the hallway where the stairs were located, he looked at Louise a bit bedazzled. Probably because she was beaming at him. Her smile was so wide and her eyes were glittering that bright, that even in dusky light her merriment was visible.

"So I am guessing you agree? We should take a break?"

Still lost for a proper answer, Louise let out a snort and chuckle, and let August come to his own conclusions. She was too tired to form an opinion, and maybe he was right all along. Maybe a holiday would be best. She wondered what 'best' was at this moment, for there was no doubt in her mind that their relationship could not be salvaged.

"But where would we go? Everything is bombed and deserted."

"I know just the place."

~

Limburg was everything Louise needed. For a moment. She had been to this southern province of her country before. In fact she had even lived there for a couple of years when she was at boarding school. But that was a different Limburg. This was near the border of both Belgium and Germany. And although the enemy had lived so near these villages, the war did not seem to have had a firm grip on this part of the world. In fact, it seemed as though nothing would ever have any effect on these green hills, relaxed looking villagers and bright skies. Louise wasn't a chauvinist at all. She would rather visit faraway places and surround herself with foreign languages and customs. But Limburg seemed to be exactly what she had been yearning for these last couple of months. After the party last winter, there was nothing that could get her out of her blues. Not even Gus' mischief or Betty's posh preaching. Little Frank seemed to be even more gloomy than she was. It worried her, but the GP continued to insist that all war babies seemed more out of sorts. He did not expand that observation by adding that these infants had suffered the insecurities their parents endured as well, but without the knowledge that the world could be a better and far less stressful place. That's what Louise added in her mind. Probably to soothe it.

She wondered why she was this blue this time around.

Was it the fact that she was rejected? That her marriage was over? That she did not recognise or worse, did not like the woman she had become? Whatever it was, Louise could not shake these gloomy clouds off her shoulders. For the first time she hated looking to the future. No more daydreaming about the countries she would visit or the theories she would learn. Everything seemed to frighten her.
But sitting next to August and seeing these gorgeous hills arise slowly got her calm for the first time in months.
She placed her hand on his thigh to emphasise this wonderful moment, but regretted it instantly. Not used to her touch anymore, August startled and turned the steering wheel in fright. Without realising it he drove straight onto the tiny road shoulder that had to protect the hundreds of sheep calmly grazing the fields from idiot drivers like him. Luckily for them, August found his sound mind in time and steered the 6-year-old Peugeot back onto the road. He nervously shook his head and let out an uncomfortable chuckle. He then patted her head a little too harshly and trembled:

"You would not think we were still in the Netherlands, would you darling?"

She loved him when he was this awkward. She really

did. His kind words and overall discomfort would fill her with warmth. It was moments like these when she really wished there was still some willingness left to fix their marriage. It would be so much easier to just fix what August and she had.

~

But she did not get out of bed that first day of their holiday. What had started off quite lovely, soon had turned into the regular nightmare August and Louise could not seem to cut loose from. Tired of making up excuses to August as to why she would not join him this day, she had acted like she could not speak or open her eyes due to the headache. It had felt rude, but not far off the truth either. Her body felt like it was being weighed down by numerous stones. Her back ached from lying on the soft mattress all night and all day. She could not think of anything, but instead she just slept every odd hour and read some pages of the new novel from her favourite author.

August had been gone most of the day, and for the first time in ages she did not feel the urge to pick herself up, get dressed and put on her usual bright smile. It was a comforting state, Louise thought after a while. A state that did not ask for much explanation on her part. August never really doubted her tiredness, and usually let her be whenever she had a headache or a cold. She found that incredibly odd. If it were the other way around she would have been very suspicious. For Louise never seemed to be ill or tired when she was around others. She was only unapproachable and moody when she was near him. But he kind of prided himself on that fact. For some odd reason he found it to be an act of true love. Only in his presence could Louise let go of all her social obligations and truly be herself. Which in a way was true. But how could he love this lazy, whining person? How could he find pride in having a wife who was a perfect hostess, the belle of the ball and in general a great company to be in, and yet be so out of sorts when no one else was around? To her it felt as if she could not find the energy to be a wonderful wife for August when there was no one else around. There was no pride to be found in that. Quite the opposite. Although she cherished the moments when she could just let go, not groom herself and stay in bed all day, she felt guilty a good part of the time because she was not able to pick herself up for her doting husband. It was yet another misbalance between them.

This holiday was bound to become a disappointment for both parties. The short pang of hope she felt the day before, when entering this beautiful part of the country she was born in, faded the minute they unpacked and went away for supper. In the early days, going out to dinner had been an activity they both loved and cherished. August because he could try out new wines and mingle with new acquaintances, and Louise because she could dress up and entertain August with one or more adventurous stories. They really had been at their best in those early, more carefree years. She honestly believed that with August she had finally found her safe haven. And a satisfying one too. Before August there had been many obsessions and mistakes, even though she was still quite young when she first set eyes on this intelligent businessman. The fact that he was successful and rich never was an issue for Louise. Of course evil tongues claimed that to be the sole reason she had lured him from his then fiancée. But they both knew the truth: she had loved him from the moment she set eyes on him. They were not an obvious match. Although both clumsy and awkward at times, Louise was far worldlier than August was. She guessed that to be the reason some doubted she really loved him. It had never occurred to her that people mainly doubted her feelings towards him because of her wandering eye, and his inability to see that tendency of hers. It had hurt her, for she had a deep yearning to be liked by both men and women. But eventually even the most evil critics had adjusted their views when seeing them together. And even now, with their marriage in shambles, people still thought them to be a lovely couple.

But that night no one in their circles would recognise the usually vibrant duo. They just stared at each other for minutes on end without anything to say to each other. It made August uncomfortable, Louise noticed. He kept on trying to start conversations but stopped whenever he saw her eyes wander. He tried to tell her about the paper production that had caused major problems for his printing business. He was keen to pick up the production after the war, but paper was still scarce, and he was trying to find new ways to up his production in spite of it. Usually Louise would find this incredibly important. She had always been a great help when it came to August's business. Her logical way of thinking brought logic to his scattered yet creative brain. But this night she could not keep a single train of thought. She wanted to tell him how unhappy she was in this marriage, but was afraid to. Afraid to hurt him, but even more to say these words out loud. It would mean that something had to be done. And she was much too tired to fight for anything, let alone for something as unsalvageable as their marriage.

She would definitely not find her way back to him, and he would forever wait for her in case she would. But it had become clearer by the minute that she would not return to him. The road back to their once-happy relationship seemed forever blocked. It literally felt that way to Louise. Whenever he touched her, her whole body would tense up and she would clench her teeth until he let go of her.

Louise just had fallen into a dreamless sleep when August stumbled inside. He was never a smooth operator, and entering a room gracefully was something he would never be able to do, she thought while giggling softly. Another trait they did have in common. Louise was the clumsiest woman she herself had ever met. She did go about it with charm though. Whenever she fell down or stumbled or knocked something over, she would giggle and mock herself with it. It made her lovable for both sexes. August looked red when he turned his head around the door. He had just come home after a day of cultural strolling. August did not find any joy in visiting a beach or somewhere else sunny. Instead he visited churches or museums, places that were cool even in the midst of summer. Usually, when both of them went on holiday, Louise would spend a day at the beach or would read in the sun if there was no beach, like now, while he would do his cultural rounds. She loved old churches and the history of the villages that surrounded them, as much as he did, but when on holiday Louise loved to relax like any other holiday-goer. But today, because of her mood, she had decided to stay in her cool apartment.

As August neared the bed Louise lay in, she softly stirred and touched her temples to show her husband she still suffered from a headache. She wanted to enjoy her solitude for just a bit longer. But unfortunately, he did not pick up on her plea to leave her alone for just an extra hour.

"Poor monkey," he softly whispered in her ear. She

winced, as that was what Jack had called her a couple of times. Why had August picked up on that?

"Does it hurt that much my darling?" August reacted on her wince. "Let me massage your neck for you so your muscles can relax for once."

There was no way she could refuse this offer, it made so much practical sense. August was like that. He would never erotically massage her. Well maybe if she asked him to, something she would never do, but he would never ever suggest it. But he did care for her and wanted nothing more than for Louise to feel better.

"Maybe you're right, lovely. Let's get your magic going then," she answered in a rusty voice.

He started to softly stroke her neck and Louise tensed up in a heartbeat. What was it about his touch that made her tense up this badly? It seemed that whenever August touched her he hit the wrong nerves. In a desperate attempt to set her mind on something else besides the massage, she started thinking about something else. Immediately her mind was fixed on Jack. It was kind of a default mode her whole being was in these days. But the thought of his hands on her only made matters worse. Which she could not wrap her mind around. August's touch was kind and soft and loving. There was nothing wrong with the actual pressure. And if she was brutally honest, she did not know how Jack's touch would feel. Of course she had fantasised about it numerous times. A day. But she had never actually experienced his slender fingers on her skin, the light pressure of his muscled hand palm on some place on her body besides her hand. There was no way she would know in what way August's touch would be different than Jack's. But there was no way she could combine the reality of August's massage with the erotic touches of Jack in her fantasy. There was no other option than to ask August to stop. And she really did not want to hurt his feelings. She felt guilty most of the time already, and there was no way she would be able to ask him to stop without letting him down. He had been so sensitive lately. She really did not want to worry him even more. There was one other way to stop this massage without hurting his feelings, but she actually cringed when she hit that thought. There was no way on earth she could have intercourse with him now. And there yet another pang of guilt entered her thoughts. How could she be on a holiday with her husband and not make love to him? She was lucky enough that he would never try to force the idea on her, let alone the actual deed, and that fact honestly made things even worse. She could just not understand her own feelings. Here she was with a husband she could laugh with, who respected her, thought she was bright, funny and lovely, and who would always put her first. And yet she felt miserable and continued to make

up ways to get out of this marriage. She sometimes got jealous when she heard women complain about their horrid partners. At least they had a good reason to leave them. At least they would get some understanding if they decided to leave. Not out in the open of course. It was a deadly sin to get a divorce. But still, people would whisper things like: there was really no other way, she showed us the bruises. She was deeply ashamed of herself when having these thoughts, but she could not help it. She was desperate. She sometimes even wished she was a widow. At least there was a way out then. But of course she did not want August dead. She loved him to bits, that's what made it so complicated. There was this constant feeling of unhappiness around her, and yet no reason to feel unhappy at all. She hated herself at that point. An unfamiliar emotion for Louise. She usually quite liked herself. And of course then there was Jack. Wonderful, quirky, inaccessible Jack. She could never get a hold of him. Never really find out how he really felt about her. Marie Louise sighed heavily.
"You see darling, you're relaxing already. Shall I go on a little bit longer? Get these tense muscles all soft and supple?"
Louise woke up from her daydream and slowly turned around to face her husband. "Oh my lovely, you have done enough already. I feel way better now. Let me take

a bath and then we will find some place nice to have supper. Sounds like a plan, right?"

August smiled and Louise returned his smile with a relieved sigh. "Let me draw you that bath, my darling."

While in the tub, Louise lost her train of thought again. She'd never really been a thinker, and her mind had been wrapped up in so many complicated thoughts lately, sometimes she just had to zone out. But to zone out completely seemed impossible these days. The only way to relax was to fantasise about this man who had become nothing less than an obsession. She knew it was not healthy at all. The way her mind and body conspired against her. All that was on their minds was him. Every single observation she made translated directly into a daydream about Jack. Even a tube of hand crème made her yearn for him and his dry fingers in winter. He had told her once about the painful edges around his nails that dried up in cold weather. Not because he was complaining about it. But because he had started bleeding when they had one of their much-cherished conversations. Him telling her this seemingly shallow fact about him, made her feel special. He was never really elaborate about anything that was related to solely him. He went on and on about his factory, or the fact that he had taken up woodworking. So why did Louise cherish these talks so immensely? There was no rational explanation at all. They did not discuss culture, politics or news. They had almost nothing in common, which often led to long moments of silence between them. But the tension, the chemical attraction; it made every encounter a memorable one. Every word he had said, every move he had made, they were all stored firmly in Louise's mind. And whenever she came across anything that could be remotely linked to one of these comments or actions, it led her straight back to her own little dream world. A world wherein she was indeed Jack's girl. At first, her fantasies were mainly expressions of lust. They were erotic scenes with explicit actions and steamy situations. She would blush feverishly sometimes when one of these thoughts rose to her mind in public. But lately Louise had been fantasising about actually being with him. She usually felt so safe in his presence. Which also did not make that much sense. August was someone who would keep her safe at any cost. She knew that. But Jack seemed to have a hold on her. With just one look or word he could gain the upper hand and wrap Louise around his dried-out fingers. There was no other man, or woman for that matter, who was capable of the same. Louise was simply not one to follow someone else's orders.

CHAPTER TWENTY-SIX

There was something crude about the way her body worked, Louise sighed when she took off her skirt and underwear. She looked at the delicate fabric, and carefully wiped off the excessive moisture that had formed a small round stain in her panties. She looked at the stain and felt tears burning at the back of her eyes. She felt as if her body was mocking her. How could she still yearn for his touch and form goose bumps whenever she smelt his scent? He had just told her he had no feelings for her, whatsoever. He had been clear and upfront about it, there had been no soothing words or even so much as a friendly tap on her shoulders to comfort her, as she was obviously in pain after finding out. But although her stomach had churned and her head seemed foggy, her body still reacted the same way it always did when in his presence. This stain in her panties was a painful reminder of the impact Jack had on her. No matter what he said, apparently. Louise held back her tears and was now rubbing the stain in an aggressive matter. Suddenly she felt the need to take it out on her undergarments. For it was this particular reaction of her body that had gotten her into trouble in the first place. From day one she had been sexually drawn to his unavailable nature. Later on she unfortunately started to really appreciate him and eventually, she fell in love. If she had not felt so incredibly attracted to him, she would never have put the effort into getting to know him, she figured. So she blamed her body for the mess she was in now. After a while she stopped rubbing and started clearing up the little pieces of paper that had fallen on the ground, and patiently plucked the dust like flakes from her underwear. The stain was still there but she was starting to calm down. Somewhere from the back of her mind the soothing voice she was far too familiar with started to address her. It was telling her yet again that she shouldn't worry. He did fancy her, but he thought it wrong and frightening. If only she could show him the way out of his and her marriage, he would be less scared and more willing to admit to himself, and eventually to her, that he in fact wanted nothing more from life than to spend the rest of it with her. Louise first tried to reason with this voice, but quickly gave up when she felt the pain in her stomach slowly melt away. Somewhere another, much quieter voice was warning her not to listen to this theory, but she had already pulled up her underwear and skirt, and she merrily left the public toilet she had, a few minutes ago, entered teary-eyed.

"You see," Jack noted cheerfully. "You're always fine within minutes. There's no reason to cut off all contact." That's a clear sign. The optimistic voice in her head had already found the proof it was looking for

before Louise had so much as muttered one word to Jack. He and her manic voice had found each other again, so all was right in the world. But for the first time since she had known Jack, this bond between her manic self and him became something of a worry to her.
She softly swung her hips from one side of the chair to the other. Apparently she had not removed all the pieces of toilet paper from her panties. The itching at least gave her time to think of what to say next. She could tell him how she really felt, could try to explain the pain he had caused time and time again by rejecting her the way he did, but without having any intentions of letting her go. But as usual her mind was temporarily out of order, and opening her mouth without the slightest clue of what would come out was not an option. Not this time. So they sat in silence for a while. Something that for some reason turned out to be the most pleasant moments between them.
"What is it that we have, Jack?" Louise had managed to form a sentence in her head before blurting it out.
It was Jack's turn to fall silent.
"You want to keep in touch, but what for? We cannot be friends as you are scared your wife would not approve. And besides, when was the last time we were together alone without fighting each other on every little thing the other says? I cannot bear the thought of

never seeing your face again, but honestly I can't think of one single sane reason to keep on seeing each other."

With a scrape of his voice Jack replied swiftly:

"Well. You seem to have worked it all out to a T. There is no reason for me to put in my two cents. So I guess I had better be gone."

She did not try and stop him. Too tired to start another plea, too heartbroken to hear another 'no'.

As Jack stood up he bent forward towards her. His face neared hers and without blinking once, Louise braced for what was coming. He stayed at a safe distance while blowing a string of hair away from her face. His breath felt soft and contained some of the scent that calmed her no matter what.

Louise expected a friendly goodbye, but instead he just straightened his back somewhat and turned away without looking back. Even when he left the café and passed the windows again, he did not look her way.

~

For some reason being rejected by Jack became easier to process. Well at least Louise seemed to recover from it faster. She had found a way to store all the painful comments he would make every time they met up. They had been through the same conversation on numerous occasions. For some reason either Jack or Louise came up with ways to meet each other again, although they had vowed to never see each other on purpose again. It had become second nature, coming up with an excuse to meet up. He desperately needed advice about supplies for his new kitchen, she was planning on going on a holiday to England again and wanted his tips, he was looking for some good restaurants in Tilburg for some business meals. And every time a meet-up would turn out to be an utter disappointment. With Jack leaving without turning back, and Louise trying to hold back her tears until she was back in her kitchen, where she could freely let them roll down her cheeks.

The amount of emotion she would experience whenever she was with him was close to the amount she felt whenever she was with August. Usually these feelings were on the other side of the spectrum. Irritation, despair and boredom as opposed to passion, hope…but then yet again despair. August and Louise no longer made any effort to act as a couple. Not even when there were friends around or they had a family dinner with their children.

Of course August did not mention the unthinkable: splitting up just wasn't a possibility. It literally was not, except when the Pope would approve it. So instead, he had decided to find the best possible way to arrange his life around Louise. She knew that if she were to change her mind and would be willing to invest into their marriage again, August would not hesitate to contribute. But for now, on the surface he seemed okay with their new living arrangements. Although it had not meant Louise moving permanently out of their marital bed. For some odd reason she still enjoyed feeling him crawl into bed next to her. Better yet, she still went to August whenever she was shaken to the core due to another meeting with Jack. He had always been able to make her feel safe and loved, and although she hated herself for turning to her husband when she so obviously was planning on starting a life with someone else altogether, she could not help but seek his comfort.

Of course she wasn't able to tell him exactly what was bothering her, but there was no need for any explanation. Just being near him in his study helped to soothe her pain somewhat. August was a man of habits, and she could always count on him retiring to his study after the family had their supper. When the children hadn't been born yet, he would start off his evening with a brandy and the evening paper, but his children were everything but patient and demanded his full attention until they went to bed. He did not mind being in their presence at all. Louise expected him to find some comfort in surrounding himself with people who would love him unconditionally, as opposed to his wife, who only did seem to love him whenever she was feeling at a loss. After Martha had taken the children to bed, like clockwork August would leave the dining room and lock himself in his study. Lately he had been playing his records even more loudly. Louise wasn't sure if it was meant as a way to keep her away, but she decided to ignore it either way on days when she needed him. She did, however, always knock before she came in. August did not have a lot of rules. Again he was quite the opposite from Louise, who was very strict about her own privacy and solitude. She emphasised 'own' in her head because she knew all too well that she did not have any respect for someone else's privacy, August's in particular. But August had it made it quite clear in the very early stages of their marriage that there were no boundaries or secrets in this household when it came down to him, except when it came to his study. He wasn't so much afraid that she would catch him doing something she shouldn't see, he was just a very jumpy person. Especially when he had his Der

Ring des Nibelungen on full blast. So she gladly obeyed this one rule, and never failed to knock before entering his study. If it had been him disturbing her reading or listening to her records, she would be annoyed to no end, but he always looked genuinely happy to see her face appear. He would turn down the volume and put down his evening paper, and tap his lap as if to guide her to her seat. These moments had become more and more sparse. At some point Louise thought it too selfish and hypocritical to continue this ritual.

During the last couple of visits to his study, she had contemplated once or twice telling him about her infatuation with Jack, but had immediately stored that thought, for it sounded ridiculous. But then again, he had always been more than capable of bringing clarity to her thoughts. It would be a very selfish act though, knowing that it would hurt him more than anything in the world. And what choice would he have if he knew? He could act like everything was still okay, or panic every time he would leave the house or if she were to visit Helen in Breda. She had put him through so much misery already, and she felt bad enough already. It was these thoughts that had kept Louise from telling her husband what had been occupying her very being for over a year now.

But her selfishness wasn't the only reason she had withheld this information. There was still one ritual she wasn't willing to give up just yet. She still cherished the moments they shared every morning. Neither of them claimed to be much of a morning person. It was one of the few dislikes they had in common. Although the reason varied, she guessed. Louise had never been able to get out of bed easily. Even as a little girl her parents had had to drag her out of bed to get dressed and go to school. At boarding school her sleeping habits had turned out to be a bigger problem, as she was always late to her first class, much to the dismay of the nuns. She could not help it, every morning when she woke up, she would feel like she had risen from death. It took her quite a while to adjust to the world of the living again, her father would joke whenever her teachers had commented on her tardiness in the mornings.

"Nothing a hearty breakfast or a strong cup of coffee can't fix," usually was his solution. Often followed by a quick: "And I'll tell her off when she's home for the holidays, of course."

August on the other hand had only started to dread the morning as he got older, and started drinking more and more. He was not a very healthy person physically, and the amount of alcohol he was consuming every single night did not help his overall physical state at all.

So ever since they were married, they had made it a habit to wake up slowly without putting too much pressure onto one another. Usually they recited their plans for the day and joked about something that had happened the day before. They had a lot of mutual friends, and enjoyed filling each other in on the latest gossip or anecdotes, and even discussed the letters they had received from one friend or the other. No matter how bad the state of their marriage, this tradition had stayed. It made her weary sometimes, these confusing feelings. For as soon as he would come near her to touch her anywhere else than a cuddle would allow, she would cringe and push him off of her. August on the other hand wasn't the sort of person that needed to be told something twice. After being rudely rejected by his wife once, he had never tried again. Which in return made Louise feel safe enough to keep on sleeping in the same bed as August.

It was these little things that kept her from pulling the plug on their relationship.

The fact that Jack did not want to leave his wife to run away with Louise did not seem to matter at all. In Louise's head her marriage with August had nothing to do with the love she felt for Jack. She would either find the strength and energy to leave August, or find a way to fix whatever was left of their marriage. She did not even link the two situations, which Jack found incredibly odd. He often claimed that if he were to tell her that he did want to run away with her, she would leave August in a heartbeat. He was dead wrong about that, Louise felt. Maybe she should have agreed with him to increase her changes of him actually confessing that he would love to leave everything for her, but she was done playing games. And besides, she did not really believe Jack would ever admit this to himself, let alone Louise.

So whenever her mind was spinning again, and she was tempted to run to August to confess anything and beg him for a way out, she wrote to Helen. Her dear friend did not have the solution on hand, but the mere act of writing down her feelings helped Louise to clear her mind. She needed to find some kind of logic to the words that randomly occupied her thoughts.

CHAPTER TWENTY-SEVEN

"Louise, just listen to me for once." He had his stern face on. The face he made when he was really going to hurt her. She braced herself for what was coming. She had already bargained with herself that she would not try to persuade him to decide otherwise, to try and convince him that he was interpreting his feelings wrongly. She had done that so many times before, and afterwards she felt less of a person. Less of the strong woman she in fact was. So she had decided that she would listen to his verdict one last time and let that message enter her body, mind and heart. She had always been too afraid to really take in what he was saying. "I'll never choose you, we don't work, you and I." To her it seemed like such a load of foolishness. How on earth could two people who reacted on each other the way they did, how on earth could they not work? What the hell would work then? Yes, she even swore when she thought of this. What did he think true love was? Just people kind of sharing a life because their hobbies matched? But she had told him this a thousand times, and knew all too well that he would never understand her point of view, like she would never be able to fathom his.

When she looked into his eyes again she felt scared and relieved at the same time. She had had enough. The pain she had gone through since she had first met him, it had reached its limit. She needed to hear his sobering words one last time. She might even need it in writing. But she supposed it was not really appropriate to ask for a written summary of this conversation. Immediately she chuckled, something she often did when she was nervous. He usually mistook this sudden merriment for some kind of indifference, which it absolutely wasn't. Another fact that was weird about their relationship. For some reason he could always translate her actions most accurately into her actual feelings. Except when it came to actions towards him. He was always dead wrong interpreting what she meant when aiming her words and actions towards him. It tired her to explain to him he was wrong. He was so used to being right that he simply would not take her word for it. Well, he never really took her word for anything, come to think of it.

"No matter what happens with my marriage, no matter what happens to yours, we will never work. I will never want you as my wife or my lover. I only ever wanted you as a friend, but even that seems to be troublesome. Please understand that the last thing I ever want to do is hurt you, but you need to know this, so you'll let go."

It'll be easier if I let go than if you have to, Louise

bitterly thought almost out loud. But instead she said nothing. She shrugged her shoulders and walked away. Without batting an eyelid. She had staged this little encounter with Jack. She knew exactly what she wanted to hear, and what her next moves would be. His story had not altered much since the last time he had rejected her. But the difference was that this time she had picked the date and time to be dumped. All the former times Jack had planned a meet-up with Louise, supposedly to 'do something nice' as friends, when in the end he always left saying he had no feelings for her. It had tainted every single encounter with Jack ever since she had confessed her feelings for him at the party.

But the last time he had told his little story about him and her not fitting together, something had snapped in Louise's mind afterwards. She did not know why then, and she did not know why now, but it had. So she had decided to hear his plea one last time on her terms and to then go home, draw a bath, wash away her make-up and crawl into bed with her pick-up player and her Marlene Dietrich record.

She had planned to play "Falling in Love Again" over and over again until she fell asleep. And she had promised herself that for the last time in her life she would not get out of bed until every last tear had left her eyes. After that, she would move on. Finally.

~

In the end it was discipline. No earthshattering revelation, no dramatic last goodbye. She had never been the sort of person that would force herself to do anything. Her impulsive character just could not be bothered with following any rules. Rules meant restrictions and in her mind the fact that she was a woman provided enough limitations already. But when it came to Jack she knew there was no other option than to let time do its work.
The wounds carved into every fibre of her being had to heal. And there was no way that would happen if she continued to meet with him, for seeing him would mean new wounds, and even worse, opening old ones. So she declined every party, every drink or get-together near Breda, with mutual friends or even near his relatives. Which was a new challenge altogether; people still were in the partying mood. And a party without Louise, or August for that matter, had been unthinkable. But much to her surprise, after sending out the first few RSVPs with a polite rejection, she did not feel guilty anymore or obligated to look for an appropriate excuse. Mainly because she did notice her spirits lift. Even her energy level went up for the first time since little Frank was born. After a few weeks she did not link every single incident, book, car, hairdo or man to Jack, and after a month or two there were days

that came and went without even mentioning them once to herself or Helen or little Frank. She had been trying to bond with him a little more by talking to him during the day – much to Martha's dismay, which had felt as a bonus. Frank and Louise now spent almost every day in each other's presence. But as much as she was pleasantly surprised at how much easier it had been to slowly forget about Jack, forming a bond with her youngest child seemed an impossible task. In the beginning he had cried for Martha hours on end, and when he finally had stopped wailing for that busybody, he started to ignore Louise altogether. It pained her to see him turning his tiny back to her, or walking off whenever she tried to comfort him. One day she decided to just ask him why he disliked her; after all he was an exact replica of his father, slow on the feet and quick on the tongue. He had started talking months before her other two children, and basically started with complete sentences.

"Little one, why are you so mad at me all the time?"

She had squatted down before him, and by doing so had blocked the way to the living room so he could not run away from her. Her voice was calm, but she knew she looked desperate.

"Your shoes scare me."

She was baffled. Only a child could have come up with a ridiculous response like this. She looked down at her feet, which were firmly on the ground. The only thing she had discovered to have in common with Frank, was the ability to squat with flat feet. Both mother and son weren't the most stable of people, but with their feet on the floor and their knees firmly in their arms they were as sturdy as anyone. Even when she wore heels, which was every single day. Ever since she had decided upon staying at home during the day, she had set her first rule ever: to get dressed like she would go out every day, and that meant wearing heels. Frank's explanation in hindsight was a very logical one, as his ears had been causing him huge discomfort from the very beginning.

"Because of the noise they make?"

Frank nodded his head and put his little hands on his ears. A big smile appeared on Louise's face as she shifted her weight and sat down so she could take off the burgundy pair that, despite the high heel, was actually rather comfortable. She thought of throwing them in a corner as a dramatic gesture, but came to her senses just in time. The worst thing she could do now was to make an even bigger noise. He was an odd one, this youngest son of hers, for he had no trouble at all playing in his father's study where on a regular basis, numerous opera singers were screaming at the top of their lungs. Even his brother's constant need to jab on the keys of their piano did not seem to bother him at all, but the scratching sound her heels made on the floor, caused by Louise's not-so-adept walk, was the cause of all agony.

"I promise you I will never wear these shoes in the house anymore, all right?"

Frank nodded and looked right at her. At a loss for what she should do next, she started telling him about the latest letter she had received from Helen. An unorthodox move, but she realised all too well that her parenting skills weren't as developed has her husband's. But much to her surprise, for the first time in his life Frank was visibly enjoying her company.

It did give her joy, this first successful contact with her lastborn. But it equally made her aware of her role in her household. More and more it seemed, that she was not needed at all. Gus had already entered the first stages of adolescence, and Betty had wanted to be completely self-reliant ever since she had started school. And Frank was looked after like a prince by Martha and August catering to his every need. Even August did not show any signs of needing her, of even wanting her near. No, concentrating more on her family had not provided her the peace and quiet she had expected, but instead it had exposed the problem that had been hidden from the surface due to her obsession with Jack. Louise had lost her home.

CHAPTER TWENTY-EIGHT

This time she had to go at it alone. She had thought of visiting her brother Jimmy and talking to him about a plan. A plan to get her life back on track. It had become painfully clear that there was no way back. Her relationship with little Frank had improved, and her constant presence both mentally and physically had tightened the family bonds somewhat, but it seemed the tighter her family became, the more left out she had begun to feel. With her focus on her family and her family alone, she had noticed that her children saved their stories for their father, and sometimes even Martha. Anyone really, except for her. If she asked about school or friends they would form an obligatory answer, but rarely would they enthusiastically tell her about what had happened on the playground. When Betty came home one day with a drawing of a woman in the kitchen, Louise's spirits lifted somewhat, but when she excitedly started complimenting her daughter on her drawing skills, Betty stopped her and stated stoically, "I haven't made it for you, mother; Martha always cooks."

Not true at all, Louise childishly replied under her breath. Louise had been preparing the family meals for weeks now, but Martha continued to serve them, so of course it still looked like she had done all the work.

It had become painfully clear that Louise had been made redundant in her own home. Of course she had only herself to blame, but that was neither here nor there. What was here was the decision she had made without any advice from Helen or her brother this time. Her brother would not be able to place himself in her shoes, so she saw no point in asking him. And Helen had done enough already. She did not want to put her in that position again, torn between being loyal to her friend and thus keeping all her secrets, or a stay a doting and trustworthy wife who would not keep any secrets from her husband.

So she had formed a plan by herself. She would emigrate. It sounded better than just running away. Emigrating had more of a ring to it, and felt much more like a well-thought-out plan than merely running from a situation that was unsalvageable. The problem was that she did not know to which country she should emigrate, and how she would move all her belongings without arousing suspicions. Well at least thinking of ways to leave had given her a new focus again. And that focus helped her to find the energy, strength and the distraction to ignore the fear that was building up inside her. Of course, she had always prided herself on being a rebel of some sort, but the harsh reality was that she had been a wife and a mother for well over 14 years. The unknown had never before felt so empty, so terribly frightening, but that encouraged her even more to go through with the plan. Never again did she want to feel incapable of change, never again did she want to be so stuck in a rut that continuing a boring life seemed better than breaking out of it.

Switzerland seemed a rather safe option. She had heard about a special hospital that was designed as a hotel. The main goal of the hospital was to relax and rest the patients. She could tell August she would go there for her headaches, and she could figure out how to move on from there. As soon as the brochure she had requested would arrive, she would tell August and pack her bags…were it not for another letter that arrived just days before the Swiss brochure.

~

Marie L.,
As you know I am awful with words. I don't even read much, as I don't have the patience to wait a couple of days to know the end of a story. I don't write if I don't have to. So the fact that I am writing this letter should warn you that this is going to be a once in a lifetime experience. Next week I will leave for South Africa. I have been planning for months to open a factory there and in a couple of weeks this dream is going to be a reality. It will be something to look forward to after the war and the dark times that followed. I don't know if we will ever see each other again, but it does feel as a definite goodbye, this trip. Not only from you but I have decided to annul my marriage to Wendy as well. We married during the war, so it should not be too much of a hassle. You know that last year has not been an easy one for me. The end of the war should have been a good thing and of course it was, but it did give me an awful lot of time to think. And lately it has become clear why we have been in this toxic relationship. I know you must be wondering if it is really me who is writing this letter, but hear me out. I know I have been obnoxious and convinced of my own right. Convinced of the fact that one could live one's life according to their own rulebook. How that must have frustrated you, knowing, not just feeling that

MARIE LOUISE

I did love you all along.
No doubt you have looked back at our short history and regretted some actions or words aimed at me. The same goes for me. And if I could, I would take it all back. In hindsight I had two options back when I first met you: I should've either left you alone immediately or seriously investigated why you had gotten under my skin so easily. Looking back I know now that the first option was never a realistic one. I think I realised this the last time we saw each other and Fons jokingly asked if you had developed some feelings for me. Never realising he was spot on. When you looked me in the eye and told me I was the love of your life, I knew. I had not seen or talked to you in over 6 months and still I felt that my feelings for you had not dialled down one little bit.
And that's the trouble with you, madam. Whenever you are near me I start to feel all kinds of emotions. And let me tell you, they're not all flattering. I have honestly contemplated pushing you out of a moving car more than once. But even more frightening: I seem to lose all control the closer I get to you. I don't have any power over anything I want, say or do, and usually I regret my actions later. To me this is not a healthy basis to build a relationship on. I have wondered on numerous occasions why you did see us together in the future. You have admitted to feeling the same sense of losing

total control when you see me. How would it ever be possible for us to start a relationship when neither of us has any kind of control over our actions? We are both intelligent, sociable people and can't afford to switch each other off? The reason I have decided to write this down anyway is that I sincerely would like to know if you have a solution to this obvious hurdle. The past couple of months were ok without you, I will not lie, but the fact that my feelings haven't faltered one little bit has made me decide to do something about it. But I really do not have a clue where to begin. Not one single clue.
That's why I have decided to write you this letter, as a goodbye. Or a start.
Sorry.
Sorry that I opened up my arms but closed them again before you reached me.
Sorry that I came looking for you when you were trying to get over me, and pulled you back into our toxic little world.
Sorry that I don't have the guts to stand in front of your house and take you away with me.
Sorry that I am not the man who can offer you what you need.
Sorry.
Forever yours,
Jack

CHAPTER TWENTY-NINE

Not until the door had opened and closed again, and the silent house at once was filled with laughter and footsteps, did Louise notice she was still sitting on top of the stairs. No one had seen her sitting there with a crumpled piece of paper still tightly in her hand. The sun had already set, and the hallway was dark except for one ray of light coming through the window of Gus' room. It shone directly on the words she had been reading frantically for hours. The ink had begun to fade already, for she had run her fingers under the words on the paper like a child learning to read a new sentence in his first book. It had been the first time in weeks that she had dared to look at the name Jack. She simply had not allowed herself to think of him, or even mention anything that had to do with him or his name. The contents of the letter had been earthshattering. An unfitting word, for she had used it before, and nothing she had experienced before resembled anything like the sensation she was feeling right now. At first she had been sensible, determined to not let the words get to her, but then her thoughts started to spiral out of control. Every single emotion she had blocked these last couple of months came tumbling out of her like bullets out of a machine gun. Her body had started to shake heavily, and her trembling fingers had lost control of the letter multiple times. Her sensible first reaction had been to burn the letter and ignore the contents, but as she had walked up the stairs to the fireplace in Martha's room, her mind had given in to severe shock the words had caused. He was emigrating, he was divorcing his wife, he was sorry. Her legs followed her mind, and when she had reached the top of the stairs she'd practically collapsed on the top step. Then, before even noticing she was crying, tears ran down her cheeks onto her knees. Little round circles appeared on her black stockings, and for a while it soothed her just watching them disappear.

I could go after him, she had whispered after a while, but immediately had cast away that thought, for she wanted to stand her ground and not fight for him anymore. Unable to hold a single line of thought, she had no other option but to stay on top of the stairs hugging her knees and praying that some clarity would enter her mind soon.

After her family had come home, Louise stood up and rubbed her sore thighs and knees. Without giving it another thought she crawled into bed, fully clothed, and closed her eyes, Jack's letter tightly tucked underneath her blouse.

~

The next morning Louise got up, changed, and grabbed the biggest handbag she could find. A toothbrush, her blush and lipstick, some underwear, Jack's letter and Rebecca by Daphne du Maurier disappeared into the old brown leather bag. The doors to the rooms of her sleeping children were firmly closed; only Martha's door stood ajar. She threw one last glance at the room August and she had slept in side by side for 14 years, and softly descended the stairs she had cried on last night. One last look in the mirror made her throw her hairbrush into the hideous bag as an afterthought. When she put on her coat she startled. Martha was up. Hastily she threw her keys onto the vanity under the mirror in the hall, and she pushed open the door. "No matter what happens," Louise said out loud when she felt the door close shut behind her, "from today on, I will be fine."

MIEKE VAN POLL

Printed in Great Britain
by Amazon